# ROLLO MICHAELS:
# THE LAST CASE

Prepared for publication by:

Authoraide Publications, LLC
1603 Capitol Ave, Suite 310 A275 Cheyenne, Wyoming 82001
Office: (307) 459-1803 | Fax: (307) 224-8450
Website: www.authoraide.com

# DEDICATION

This book is dedicated to all my
brothers and sisters of the badge
who took the oath to
protect and serve.
Sadly, too many gave their all.

# ACKNOWLEDGMENTS

**AS MY EYESIGHT** continues to diminish, my computer screens get bigger while my doctors try the latest meds to slow down the inevitable. Therefore, without the help of a number of people, I couldn't get any writing done.

Unlike me, my computer isn't a simple tool. As a self-published author, what worked seven years ago is no longer possible. I wish to thank computer guru, Joe Fryman, for his incredible patience in helping my computer work for my particular needs. Joe has taught this old dog new tricks.

Vision issues had me try something new with this book: a publishing manager/helper. Thank you, Marcus Webb, for your help with KDP. If there are any errors, I'll blame them on you.

And special thanks to the Rollo Michaels Fan Club members on Facebook who keep asking for more about him. It's why I didn't kill him off!

# Epigraph

*" The flapping of a butterfly's wings*

*deep within the Amazon Jungle,*

*can cause a hurricane in China."*

- Chaos Theory

*"Shit happens!"* — Rollo Michaels

# PROLOGUE

**THE RINGING PHONE** on my nightstand got me elbowed in the ribs. Usually, the love of my life isn't that rough, but our colic-prone baby daughter was causing her mom severe sleep deprivation. I snatched the phone from the nightstand and fled the room. The screen lit up with the name Brandon, my only son.

"What?" I said.

"We need you here, right away. Mom and her boyfriend got into it. The asshole punched her in the face and took off. She took out her gun and capped two at him. Should I call the cops?"

"Jesus! Did she hit him?"

"She doesn't know, Dad, but she's a wreck. I don't know what to do. Hurry, please!"

"See you in fifteen minutes. Put your mother on the phone," I said, putting my cell on speaker so I could pull on my jeans while listening to my son trying to get Marie on the phone.

Our baby daughter started to cry.

"You woke up the baby. What's going on?" Linda shouted.

"She won't talk. She's bleeding from her nose and mouth," Brandon said as Linda entered the living room, carrying our baby.

"Who?" Linda mouthed. "Marie?"

I nodded and watched her face go from anger to concern. I pulled my hoodie over my head, phone in one hand, keys in the other, heading to the car, keeping my son on the line.

"You're going there?" Linda said, quickly grasping the obvious.

"To calm things down. Get back to bed, sweetheart."

"Dad, you there?"

"Yeah, son."

"The police just pulled up."

"Get your mom's gun and put it in the oven." That made Linda's eyes and mouth open wide.

"The oven?" my son asked.

"Yes. Hide it until I get there. I'll be there in ten minutes. Tell the officers who your father is and nothing else. Tell your mother not to say anything. Got it?"

"Okay. The police are knocking on the door. Should I let them in?"

"Hide the gun first. Tell the officers what happened, but don't mention the shooting!"

Brandon's mother is my ex-wife of seven years. We married twice and divorced twice. We had two children from our first go-round, but the scars of old wounds doomed our second attempt. Brandon's older sister, Melissa, is a UCLA sophomore. My current and hopefully last wife, Linda, is the mother of my youngest daughter, three-month-old Marlowe. All this ran through my head on the trip to the house I paid for.

Flashing reds and blues lit up the cul-de-sac. I parked in the neighbor's driveway and ran to the house. The uniform on the door blocked my entry until Brandon shouted, "Dad!' The crew of the rescue unit was administering to my ex. The sergeant in charge recognized me.

"Hey, Michaels, long time no see."

"Hello, Bart. I see they'll make anybody sergeant," I said. And it got me a smile and the finger.

"We're taking her to the ER. She needs stitches on her lip," the attendant said as he and his partner helped Marie to her feet and guided her to the ambulance.

"My son and I will follow," I said.

"We need to talk to your boy, Rollo. Your neighbor called in a shots fired call, and it doesn't take Dick Tracy to recognize the two bullet holes in the front door. Your son said he wanted you here before answering any questions, and we couldn't get anything from your ex," Bart said.

"We got a blood trail leading to the street, Sarge," an officer shouted through the open front door. *It was getting complicated.*

# CHAPTER 1

## FOUR MONTHS LATER

**YESTERDAY, A JURY** of four men and eight women was sworn in. I missed the two-day contentious jury selection battle, but my business partner and now my ex-wife's attorney, Art Salazar, said he was more than happy with the outcome.

"All rise!" the bailiff announced, signaling the entrance of the judge with her flowing hair and robe. When she sat, the bailiff continued, "Department 104 of the Superior Court of Los Angeles County is now in session, Judge Amanda Carson presiding. Be seated."

"Will the defendant please rise," Judge Carson said. I watched my ex-wife rise in unison with her attorney. "In the case of the People vs. Marie Michaels, Defendant is charged with attempted murder under Penal Code Sections 664/187(a). How does the defendant plead?"

"Not guilty, Your Honor," Art replied.

"Is that correct, Ms. Michaels? You wish to plead not guilty?" Marie nodded in the affirmative, causing Art to whisper in her ear. Marie's shakily voiced, "Yes, Your Honor," was barely heard by those sitting behind her.

"So entered," the judge said. "Are the people ready for their opening remarks?"

"Yes, Your Honor," the deputy prosecutor said, as Art and my ex took their seats.

Marie turned and spotted me, Brandon, and Melissa seated in the first row behind the defense table. We nodded and smiled our encouragement, bringing a tight-lipped smile to her face.

"Ladies and gentlemen of the jury, the people will show…" and Deputy DA Cora James laid out her case. My business partner, Arturo Salazar, had spent seven years in the District Attorney's office, sitting at the other table, prosecuting hundreds of cases. He was representing Marie pro bono. My business, Michaels & Associates, started out with two ex-cop private investigators and Art, my divorce attorney, to keep us out of trouble. We morphed into a private security company with a "Have Gun, Will Travel" mojo appealing to those who thought defunding the police was a good idea they could afford.

Twenty-five minutes later, Cora James finished a lengthy explanation of what the people would show to prove the elements of the attempted murder charge. It was Art's turn, and he stood. In a confident voice, he said, "Your Honor, the defense waives opening remarks at this time." His statement caused a stir at the prosecution table.

Detective Joe Roberts of Valley Bureau Homicide got up from the table and left the courtroom to fetch the alleged victim who had suffered two gunshot wounds, one in the shoulder and one in the ass. *I had taught Marie and our kids to shoot very well.*

Roberts hurried back to their table. A brief exchange had the Deputy DA shaking her head and the detective shrugging his shoulders. "Your Honor, the People request a ten-minute recess as we attempt to locate our first witness."

Now it was the judge's turn for head shaking. "Let's take ten. Both counsel to my chambers. Now!" A flourish of robe and hair hurried from the bench, Cora James and Art Salazar dutifully following. Detective Roberts dashed from the courtroom to begin his search for the missing witness.

When I approached the rail separating the legal arena from the unwashed, the bailiff gave me a fish-eyed stare to ensure I wasn't slipping Marie a gun or handcuff key. I waved, exposing both my empty hands.

"How are you holding up, Marie?"

She turned to me. "Facing five to life has my panties knotting up. I don't think the kids should be here to hear all this."

"Art does. He wants to show your human side to the jury."

"What's that supposed to mean?" she snapped.

"Family support and shit like that," I said, taking the discourse to a lower level. Melissa instinctively interrupted our about-to-be sparring session.

"What's going on with the judge and lawyers, Mom?" she asked.

"I have no idea. What do you think?" Marie asked me.

"I think your boyfriend chickened out."

Homicide detectives have an aversion to coincidences and surprises, because they get in the way and make more work. I've known Joe Roberts going back many years. We were never friends, but we had a history. His arrogance kept him from being a team player, and few wanted to partner with him. I haven't had contact with him since leaving the LAPD but often read about him solving another murder in the newspapers.

Roberts was a college grad with a little over twenty-five years of service on the department, nine as a Homicide Dick. While the department was promoting many of his peers to lieutenant and captain, Joe was solving murders. And he was one of the best at it, so he never devoted his time studying for promotional exams. Instead, he spent his time checking files, reviewing forensic reports, and interviewing witnesses and suspects. Many detectives envied his *cleared-by-arrest* rate. Known within the fraternity as "The Lone Wolf," Roberts went through partners like Kleenex. Known as Joe's Go-fers, none lasted more than a few months before asking for a different partner or a transfer. His boss tried to implement a rotating slot for all newbies coming to the unit, but the top brass soon squelched it.

Ten minutes slowly turned to twenty before the bailiff removed the jury. Ten more passed before Art and the prosecutor returned to their respective tables to shuffle papers into folders. Another five and the judge returned to the bench. Her expression said, "Unhappy," her voice said court would reconvene at 9:00 a.m. tomorrow.

Art informed us that Detective Roberts couldn't produce the supposed victim, Ernest Palmer, and the judge had issued a body attachment for him. Art explained that the judge might dismiss the case if the victim isn't located by tomorrow. He added that Roberts explained he just found out his partner called off sick this morning and failed to ensure Palmer was in court on time. The judge opined that was a lame excuse.

O   O   O

The drive home from the courthouse was mainly silent before I turned on my radio and played some '70s music on K-Earth 101. Brandon rode shotgun, and Marie and Melissa enjoyed the view from the back seat. Each time I checked my rearview mirror, Marie glared at me. When I returned my eyes to the road ahead, I could still feel her eyes. I knew this ordeal was eating away at her soul and felt for her. She seemed to have aged ten years in the past four months. I was grateful for Linda's understanding when I told her I was picking up the tab for Art's time away from Michaels & Associates.

As we drove west on Victory Boulevard, the radio had Bob Dylan "Knockin' on Heaven's Door." And the tears started to flow, first Marie, then Mel, then Brandon, and finally, me. I was overcome with guilt as I asked myself, *Is all this pain my doing?*

"How 'bout lunch at Brent's Deli on Parthenia? I'm starving," I said.

"Me too, Dad," was Brandon's response. Melissa remained silent as if waiting for her mother to speak first.

"You all know I got this damn thing around my ankle as part of my bail agreement, don't you? Better take me home first," Marie said.

"You're going home from court, and I had to stop on the way," I said, turning north and heading to Brent's.

"We all have to eat, Mom," was Melissa's vote of approval.

Brent's never fails to please. This was our first meal together in more than a year, and just the four of us alone in more than three years. Divorce has a way of doing that.

Table conversation was light, and we avoided talking about the trial entirely. Surprisingly, Marie asked how Linda and baby Marlowe were doing. I took out my phone and let her scroll through about a hundred baby pics.

"She looks a lot like you, Mel," Marie said.

"Ya think? After all, she *is* my sister."

# CHAPTER 2

## ENOUGH PAIN

**THE NEXT MORNING,** our entourage remained in the hallway outside the courtroom door of Dept. 104 while Marie's attorney met with the judge in chambers. Left to speculate on what was going on inside, I could see Marie's angst building. Knowing her for over twenty-five years, I could tell she hadn't slept much last night.

Art came out to fetch his client. He looked ruffled, like a guy who lost an argument, prompting me to ask, "What's going on?"

"You can all come in now," he said, holding the door for Marie and the kids. He grabbed me and whispered, "According to Joe Roberts, Ernie Boy got himself murdered." We followed Art in, taking the same seats we had yesterday. Detective Roberts sat next to the dressed-to-impress deputy DA. The shock of what Art told me buzzed in my head. Pondering how much a young trial attorney got paid or why Detective Roberts chose to share his hard look with me, didn't help. *What did I do, Joe?*

"Will the defendant please rise," Judge Carson said. "Ms. Michaels, because of the untimely death of the prosecution's key witness, I am dismissing the charges against you without prejudice. That means the district attorney is free to pursue this case at another time. I now revoke your house arrest, order your bail money to be returned, and you are free to go."

Marie sagged and Art guided her back into her seat "Your Honor," he said, "For the record, I wish to state the defense's objection to the without prejudice clause of the dismissal, and that my objection made part of the record," Art said.

"So noted, Mr. Salazar. Court is adjourned." And she banged her gavel and swooshed to her chambers, hopefully never to be seen again by Marie.

As Marie hugged the kids and thanked Art, Roberts snuck up behind me and tapped me on the shoulder. "We need to talk, Michaels."

"About what?"

"The shooting death of your ex-wife's boyfriend, Ernie."

"No thanks. I'm guessing you think my ex got it right this time?" I asked, smiling.

"Or maybe you or your son. Did you know your boy told me he hid the gun from the coppers at the scene that night?"

"Yeah, I told him to. I know you ran with this bull-shit case only because you hate my guts. If you think one of us did that asshole, prove it. Did he eat his gun?"

"How'd you know that?" his raised voice, drawing attention, causing Art to quickly step between us.

"Lucky guess," I said as Art pushed me toward the family group.

"What was that about?" Art asked.

"We had a dustup back in the day."

"You have a history with Roberts and didn't think to tell me about it?"

"I have a history with a lot of people." I added, "I figured Marie's case was a no-brainer," and raised Art's hackles, my smile not placating my partner. *My bad.*

I gave the kids a goodbye hug. Melissa would drive her mom and brother home. After telling Art I'd see him back at our offices, I went to my car and found Detective Roberts leaning up against it, smoking a cigarette. His scowl was saying he wasn't enjoying his day. "Don't you know those things will kill you?"

"You're an asshole, Michaels, always was, always will be."

"You trying to butter me up?"

"Can you account for your time and whereabouts the night before last?"

"Yes."

"Yes? Yes, what?"

"Yes, I can account for my whereabouts the night before last, but I don't want to tell you shit."

Joe Roberts lost it. He did a two-handed grab of my jacket lapels and got up in my face. With tobacco breath and undertones of coffee, he sneered, "I think you're good for this, Michaels, and I'm going to—"

I stopped him midsentence using a twist-lock technique on his wrist to drop him to his knees and then reversed it to put him on his face. My triumph was short-lived as all hell broke loose. Two blue suits were on me like stink on you know what. A quick beat down had me face-planted in asphalt as over four hundred pounds of LA's finest landed on me as if they'd jumped from the courthouse roof. They quickly cuffed my hands behind my back. My pride was hurt, but I had suffered worse indignities. I should have known Roberts wouldn't have gotten physical without backup.

At least it was a short walk to the Van Nuys jail. Roberts wanted to hum me in on a bullshit battery on a police officer charge. It was a good thing I safely hid my gun in a lockbox welded to the floorboard of my car or else my bail would've cost me a week's pay.

They stood me upright then helped Roberts to his feet. His thumb pointed in an odd direction as he gripped his left wrist to his chest, his face twisted in pain. He sneered, "You broke my wrist! You'll pay for this, asshole."

The pain in my back seemed like payment enough.

# CHAPTER 3

## ANOTHER ARREST

**_I WAS COOLING_** down in an interrogation room instead of a holding cell, still tightly cuffed, and left to admire my profile in the two-way mirror. The road rash on the left side of my face oozed and burned, but my reflection told me it wouldn't spoil my good looks.

I did a Houdini, slipping my cuffed hands under my butt and removing the handcuff key hidden in my left shoe. *Click-click*, and the cuffs were off. I handcuffed the two metal chairs in the room together to give Roberts more grief then stepped out into the bullpen and headed toward the lieutenant's desk, rubbing the cuff marks on my wrists.

"Hey, if it isn't Rollo Michaels! What brings you to Van Nuys dicks?" Lieutenant Bill Dacey asked. He had been one of my sergeants when I worked a central patrol car a lifetime ago.

"Two uniformed officers per the insistence of your boy, Joe Roberts."

"He's not my boy. Roberts works homicide. What's up?" His smile flashed.

"I want to make a personnel complaint against Detective Roberts," I said, wiping the smile from Bill's face. "Who's his captain?"

"Malinka. Where's Joe?"

"Getting x-rays. I think I broke his wrist."

"Not funny, Michaels."

"It's the truth, Bill."

Shock registered on his face as he picked up the phone. He punched in the captain's extension, and requested an audience, and we went to see Captain Malinka. When I first set eyes on her fifteen years ago, Corinne Malinka was a boot right out of the police academy. She was a looker then and, at thirty-seven, was still a head-turner. She eyeballed me up and down as me and Bill Dacey stood before her desk.

"What happened to your face, Michaels?"

"A little dustup with Joe Roberts, Captain," I said and sat without an invitation, the lieutenant following my lead. I gave her the five-minute version of my ex-wife's case and my belief Joe Roberts's relentless quest was based on the bad blood that flowed between us. Of course, she wanted full disclosure, and I complied.

"When Roberts and I were assigned to Wilshire Detectives about ten years ago he, homicide, me, robbery, my marriage was down the tubes. With a divorce in progress, I was seeking love in all the wrong places and was hit upon by a twenty-something from Playa Del Rey. A why-not attitude had me spend a weekend in her apartment, the view of the Pacific from her balcony was not what kept me there. She had a fight with her boyfriend a few days before, and I was the vehicle for her revenge. Sadly, the boyfriend was none other than Joe Roberts, and she gladly told him of our tryst." During the telling, Captain Malinka leaned forward in her chair to read my facial expressions and gage my truthfulness.

Her tactic, taught in most interrogation classes made me uncomfortable, but I continued. "Joe didn't take it well and confronted me in the back of the police station. I spotted the roundhouse sucker punch coming while he was still thinking of it, stepped inside, and hip-rolled him to the ground, then bitched-slapped him. A uniformed sergeant intervened while several officers stood by, cheering us on."

Captain Malinka shook her head and was about to delve deeper into my story when a commotion arose in the detective squad room. One of them stuck his head into Captain Malinka's office door and informed us, "Boss, a prisoner has escaped from an interrogation room!"

"No, Corrie, I'm right here," I said and raised my hands.

$$\circ \quad \circ \quad \circ$$

Telling my side of the encounter with Roberts got me eyebrow raises and headshakes but no follow-up questions. Instead, as I waited to be led away, she conferred with Dacey and Roberts's boss, Lieutenant Fred Simms, as if I wasn't in the room.

"Based on what the officers told me, I approved the booking for battery on a police officer. We held off on the booking until Roberts returned from the hospital," Simms said.

At that time, they received word from the emergency hospital that Roberts was being prepped for surgery, and Malinka dispatched Simms to interview Roberts. Simms left, and Malinka ordered Dacey to return me to the interview room after I promised to behave myself. Knowing me as she did, she told Dacey, "Make sure you lock the door, Bill."

"Say, Cap. You should probably have Dacey talk to the uniforms who took me down before Roberts or Simms do," I said. "I know how things sometimes get spun to fit certain narratives. Why were the two coppers hanging out, waiting for a bus?" She made a sour face and told Dacey to bring the two officers to her office with their reports after booking their prisoner.

While escorting me back to the interview room, Dacey told me of Simms's well-known disdain for Joe Roberts, but putting Joe in the hospital meant I wasn't going home anytime soon.

Things moved faster, and I was soon strip-searched, booked, printed, and smiled for my photos. Word travels fast in the *Land of the Blue*, and several old acquaintances came by, some to say hi, some to mock me. But mostly, they just looked and shook their heads.

Of course, my first phone call after being booked for a felony battery charge was to my lawyer and business partner, Art Salazar. He thought I was pulling his leg, but when I told him the particulars, he went ballistic. The bondsman was at the Van Nuys jail a half-hour before Art. More than five hours had passed since Joe Roberts had grabbed hold of my suit jacket.

"You look like crap!" was Art's hello. "He do that to your face?"

"No, actually, it was two uniforms. I think he had strategically placed them as part of the ambush," I said as Art took some photos of my face with his phone.

"We're going to get you checked out at the hospital," Art, the lawyer, said. "Anything else hurting besides your pride?" Art, my friend and business partner, asked.

Going to the same hospital where Joe Roberts was getting his broken wrist and dislocated thumb fixed wasn't the smartest of choices, but it was the closest to the Van Nuys jail. Roberts's boss, Lieutenant Simms, was pacing the lobby when Art and I walked in.

"What are you doing here?" he shouted.

I said, "Thought I'd check on Detective Roberts," which only got me a frown and a headshake.

# CHAPTER 4

## LOVE'S ANGUISH

***I AWOKE THE*** following day with a muffled groan and slid out of bed, trying not to disturb sleeping beauty. Linda had been up half the night with our colicky baby daughter. The clock said 7:00.

The urine sample jar sat atop the toilet tank, awaiting my morning duty call. The emergency room doctor who discovered the bruising on my back and around my kidneys gave me specific instructions on how to pee in the jar as if I were a moron. I stood there waiting for inspiration: *Tick-tock, tick-tock.* Time was a-wasting, and I had a nine o'clock follow-up appointment. Just when I started to go, my phone rang. It went to voice mail as I went in the jar. My pee was an Amber Bock, not a Pilsner Light. Not good. I screwed the lid on and washed my hands. I fired up a dark roast pod in the kitchen to treat my funk. As the aroma of the best thing to come out of Columbia before cocaine, I hit the play button on my cell.

"Hey, Boss, you're all over the internet, throwing some old guy to the ground then getting your ass kicked by the boys in blue. I think you need more time in the dojo," said my IT man and resident black-belt bouncer Emanuel Hemmings at Michaels & Associates. "I'm sending you a copy."

I watched as Joe Roberts grabbed me and got in my face, me breaking his grip and twisting him to the ground as two officers tackled me from behind. Two knee bombs took the fight out of me, and the cuffs went on. They stood me up, but Roberts remained on the ground, holding his arm and writhing in pain. Thankfully, there was no sound. The video meant the humbug arrest wouldn't go anywhere. My coffee tasted even better than it smelled.

My cranky daughter's cries of hunger were Linda's wake-up call, and she shuffled into the kitchen with Marlowe in her arms. "Did I hear your phone ringing?"

"Yep, Manny had something important for me."

"That couldn't wait 'til eight?" was more a statement than a question.

"I'm going to the shower," I said as Linda put a pan of water on the stove to heat our little girl some formula, the current baby-formula shortages notwithstanding.

o  o  o

The doctor said nothing to surprise me: there's blood in my urine, drink plenty of water, no alcohol for a week, and drop off another urine test in three days. I passed on visiting Joe Roberts in his hospital room, thinking he might have a gun under his pillow. I took my new sample jar and left, heading to Michaels & Associates via the Hollywood Freeway. It was almost 10:45 when I got there. Ruth told me two officers from LAPD were waiting in our conference room enjoying coffee.

"Is Art in?" I asked.

"He called, said he should be here before eleven," Manny said from behind the computer screen array on his desk. "You look at the video I sent?"

"Yes, and me thinks that's why we have LAPD guests drinking our coffee."

"What video?" asked Ruth.

Manny looked at me for an okay, and I did a subtle negative headshake.

"Sorry, Ruth, but if I show it to you, I'd have to kill you," he said, causing Ruth to respond with a middle finger salute. "Tell Art about my visitors and send him right in when he gets here, and play nice, children. Manny, turn on the recorder, please. You can shut it off when Art joins me." And I went to the conference room.

"You guys save me any coffee?" I said, going for the pot on the cart. They had. Both stood as I poured a cup and offered them more. They declined and offered their hands to show they didn't hold knives.

"I'm Lieutenant Ratcliff, from LAPD's Office of the Inspector General," he said as we shook. "And this is Sergeant Silverman of Internal Affairs Group. The sergeant's dead fish was sweaty and weak, even for a small woman, which she wasn't. She remained silent, her expression blank. When I let go, she wiped her hand on her jacket sleeve.

"Please have a seat. I should tell you up front Michaels & Associates doesn't do divorce cases, so how can I help you?" The sergeant bristled, and the forced smile on the lieutenant's face disappeared.

"Your attempt at humor is not appreciated, Michaels. You know damn well why we're here," Ratcliff snapped.

"I'm just trying to kill a little time while we wait for my attorney to get here, Lieutenant. You know street coppers call you Ratso, don't you?" I said to knock him off his high horse.

His face lit up like it was on fire. "You listen here! Nobody puts one of our people in the hospital without paying the price. I can make your life miserable to no end, get your license pulled—get your concealed carry revoked."

"Everything alright in here, Rollo?" Art said, walking in, carrying his empty briefcase as a prop. "Sorry to keep you waiting. As you know, traffic is terrible."

"We came here in good faith to see if the charges against your client could be dropped because of some exculpatory evidence that has come to light," Ratcliff said, "but Michaels has resorted to name-calling and working on his comedy act."

"And I thought you were here to investigate Mr. Michaels's complaint against three officers for assaulting him under the color of authority," Art said.

"That's bullshit, and your client knows it. He baited Detective Roberts into a confrontation, and Roberts attempted to detain your client for questioning," Sergeant

Silverman injected. By finally saying something, she gave away their strategy.

"So much for an open-minded investigation. We're done here for now. Perhaps you two should watch the five o'clock news tonight. Feel free to come back when you have your facts straight," I said.

"You going to the press?" Ratcliff asked as he and Silverman stood.

"No, but a concerned citizen has dropped another video bomb on LAPD. Might be time to circle the wagons instead of trying to intimidate this old cop, Ratso. I hear you're about to make Captain. You screw this up, what happens?"

"Screw you, Michaels," he said, and they left.

"WTF, Rollo! You're going to tell me, right?" I took out my phone and showed him the video. He replayed it three times then opined, "This changes everything. Where's the audio?"

"No clue."

o   o   o

When I arrived home from the office, Linda sat on the couch in front of our 55-inch TV. The *News at Six* talking heads made no sounds. A sleeping Marlowe lay on a blanket, snuggled up beside her, and our cat, El Gato, sought my attention by rubbing against my ankles. A box of tissues was on Linda's lap and some used ones were scattered on the floor by her feet. She turned toward me as if to speak. Her tearstained face and red-rimmed eyes spoke of her pain and anguish. Feelings of guilt flooded me for keeping the events of yesterday from her.

Another tear ran down her cheek as our eyes met. "Oh, Rollo, I just can't do this anymore."

# CHAPTER 6

## HOME FRONT

**OUR PLANS FOR** Saturday and Sunday had been in place for over a week, and Linda refused my offer to cancel. Melissa and Brandon were due at one o'clock to spend the weekend with their baby sister and us. Pool time and Dad's famous BBQ ribs were the additional attractions. Today's rain, the first in a month, wasn't the only thing threatening quality family time. All my sorry excuses, pleas for forgiveness, and promises to do better didn't stack up against Linda's litany of complaints. Each one was a painful recital of the pain I caused her.

"Another arrest, another beat down. What about Marlowe if, God forbid, you don't come home to us? All your macho bullshit and ego-driven mistakes—I can't be an enabler while you put yourself out there for someone other than your own family." She ended her stinging rebuke by giving me her two-week notice, quitting her post at Michaels & Associates. My other partners, Clancy and Art, would not welcome this news.

"Why are you dumping on me like this? It's not a good time, sweetie. It was because of my family I'm in this mess. Detective Roberts is trying to hang a murder on your husband, and I'm not laying down for him. Is this some post-partum thing going on?" I realized I shouldn't have said the last part when she stormed off to the kitchen. Aches, pain, and anger were overriding my inner moderator.

I started after her when a ringing phone saved me from digging a deeper hole for myself. I picked up without looking at caller ID. My "Hello?" probably sounded insincere.

"I see where my detective made you a TV star," Captain Malinka said.

"I told you what went down. You see anything in the video that makes me a liar?"

"Can't say that I did. Why didn't you say something about the recording?

"I didn't know. My lawyer's thinking a six-figure settlement with no decimal points between the digits. Then yesterday, two Internal Affairs people showed up at my business to try their intimidation ploy, which probably gets a lot of confessions from newbies."

"Now you're suing? Why, because your feelings were hurt?"

"No, because I'm pissing blood!"

"You should know the two officers said Detective Roberts asked them to stand by because he thought you might resist arrest, and they wrote it up that way."

"You talked to them, and they said Roberts intended to arrest me? And they wrote it up in their arrest report?" I asked.

"Yes, Rollo."

"Things have radically changed since I left the department. Back then, you needed probable cause to arrest someone. When did it change?"

O   O   O

The rest of the weekend passed without drama. My kids were not asking anything about the incident in the courthouse parking lot, as if they hadn't seen the video. Baby Marlowe got most of their attention with Melissa even taking a few naps with her sister. But they thought my swimming in a T-shirt was weird, not knowing about the ugly bruising the shirt hid.

My Monday doctor's visit was not the formality I expected. My urine specimen still didn't please the doc, and he had me sent to imaging for an ultrasound. But that wasn't his only bad news for me: I had cracked ribs, again, a third time for these two ribs. When told of the previous cracks and scars associated with these injuries, the doc wanted to shave me and tape me up.

"Sorry, Doc, I'll wear a brace, but there's no way I'm going through that that tape thing ever again."

"I won't hurt you," he said.

"Pain I can take, Doc. All the itching is the deal breaker."

He smiled and sent the nurse for a large torso brace. Then he told me the blood in my urine was caused by trauma to small vessels in the organs and gave me another sample jar to bring back Thursday. He then helped me put my girdle on and instructions not to do this, that, and the other thing. "And don't forget, drink plenty of water and no alcohol."

"Why are you worried about my liver?"

"I think it could be bruised, after what I saw on television," he said, making a face like he had just bit into a lemon.

On the drive to the office, my resentment toward Joe Roberts continued to grow. Maybe I'll let Art file the suit. My cell rang in the cup holder. I hit the button and said, "Speak of the devil."

"What's your ETA?" Art asked.

"Ten minutes. What's up?"

"You have an alibi for the night Ernie Palmer killed himself?"

"Why would I need one?"

"Bill Dacey called me to whisper Roberts is telling anyone who'll listen, Palmer had help. He says you're a viable suspect, and you resisted his attempt to take you in for questioning."

"That's bullshit. The whole thing was a setup. The two coppers were there to back him up. You need to get a copy of the reports before they get edited."

"Edited?"

"You'll figure it out. The way it was originally written, any filing deputy in the DA's office would reject it," I said as the driver of the car in front of me slammed on its brakes.

A man, dressed only in black socks, had ran into the intersection of Hollywood and Highland. He was being chased by two of Hollywood's finest. I was a little slow on the brake and tapped the rear bumper of the more attentive driver in front of me. The driver behind me stopped and was immediately on her horn.

"Looks like I'll be later than my first estimate. Listen, Art, do me a favor and call Dacey back. Tell him we'd appreciate a copy of my arrest report and ask if Lieutenant Simms made a written report of his initial conversation with Roberts at the hospital," I said and ended the call.

The wrestling match only lasted a minute. The hot roadway had Mr. Socks screaming for mercy as the officers led him to the sidewalk to the cheers of the crowds that gathered, many with cellphones in hand. The guy I tapped pulled to the curb south of all the played-out drama. I slid in behind him as he inspected his bumper. To my surprise, he gave me the okay sign and waved me on, shattering my belief that the world is full of a-hos who come out rubbing their necks.

# CHAPTER 6

## BACK TO WORK

**MONDAYS SUCK! I** say that from a lifetime of experience. It's not Monday's fault that it follows a weekend, it just worked out that way. Sure, now and then, a Monday is a Federal holiday. Still, they usually cause more problems than they're worth, no mail, banks inconveniently closed, not to mention all the times we forget next Monday is a holiday. *Or is it the week following?*

Art was already gone when I got to the office, leaving Ruth and Manny the Nerd holding down the fort. My other partner, Clancy, was off, taking his wife to the Samuel Oschin Cancer Center at Cedars for her biweekly chemotherapy. Sylvia's two-year up-and-down battle with the disease has affected us all. This round of treatment featured a new cocktail of poisons we prayed would succeed where surgery and radiation failed.

With me late, Clancy at the hospital with his wife, Linda home teaching Marlowe the finer points of pouting, and Art mounting a vigorous defense of yours truly, there'd be no Monday associates meeting this morning.

"Ruth, will you send a dozen roses to Linda with an *I'm sorry* note?" I asked, handing her my credit card. She took it with a smile. "Linda filled you in already, I take it."

She smiled and nodded, singing, "That's what friends are for."

"And what did you do this time, Boss?" Manny asked from behind his computer array.

"Just being me has its costs."

"The *man upstairs* wants a meet with you sometime this morning," Ruth said.

"He say what about?"

"Covid vaccinations."

The *man upstairs* refers to Jack Parker, our newest crew member, and Security Services division manager. Ex-army ranger, ex-LAPD, a member of the Screen Actors Guild, a long-time gym rat, and professional wrestler Jack Parker has an impressive résumé. He is bigger than Manny by two inches and weighs a buffed 280. He makes a perfect Mister Clean impersonator, with his shaved head and hoop earring. Even after seven months, why he wants to work for us remains a mystery. I figured Jack wanted a raise after doubling our security business since coming on board.

While with the police department, Jack had a full head of hair and no earrings. He often told us he was Chief William Parker's grandson, which was bull, but his war stories were not. His campaign ribbons included a Silver

Star denoting the five major battles he fought in, plus his Bronze Star and Purple Heart medals. Me, I didn't even get a Good Conduct ribbon after my two stints.

One night, Jack answered a call to a Hollywood producer's home in Topanga Canyon. A few months later, he turned in his gun and badge, joined the Screen Actors Guild, and appeared in a made-for-TV movie. A fellow actor introduced him to a WWE promoter. Between bit parts in minor films, he toured the junior circuit of WWE, learning how to fake it until an opponent forgot the script and tampered with Jack's man parts. Jack reverted to his Special Forces training and significantly damaged the guy's facial structure. The crowd loved it, but the brass at WWE ended his career.

We're members of the same gym in the Valley on Ventura Boulevard, and he was always interested in my war stories and I, his of Desert Storm and Afghanistan. His near-death experiences outnumbered mine by five-to-one, but mine were funnier. During one of these BS sessions, he asked if Michaels & Associates could use someone of his ilk. I jumped without hesitation, and partners be damned. Art and Linda didn't have a problem, but Clancy insisted on a background check. I contacted Commander Grahek in Chief Moore's office, who pulled Jack's personnel package and told me our guy was "Eligible for Rehire." With everybody on board, Art created another Limited Liability Company installing Jack Parker as GM.

The guy filled out a thousand-dollar suit, sans tie, nicely. He replaced the gold hoop with a 3/4K diamond, reminding me of an NFL tight end. I wondered if we could really afford this guy. He extended his hand and said, "Good morning, Boss," his chemically whitened chicklets flashing. He was carrying a number of file folders in his other hand.

"Don't squeeze my hand, big guy, or I'll fire your ass. What's up?"

"I see getting your ass kicked has left you in a bad mood. I told you all those donuts would make you soft. Best be getting back to the gym." He slipped into the chair and placed the folders on my desk.

"Ruth told me you swiped a couple of my maple glazed, thus my bad mood. She also said you wanted to talk to me about Covid. You got it?"

"No, but I'm vaxxed. I guess that doesn't mean I can't get it. Some of our clients are wanting Covid vax cards for our people. Of our thirty-seven employees, ten aren't completely vaxxed. Three of them refuse any shots."

"Fire them? Cut the hours of the other seven? Restrict them to outside posts? Figure it out, Jack," I said.

"We'll be facing a lot of overtime. I'll need to hire more part-time off-duty coppers. Any ideas?" he asked.

"Ask your most trusted peeps for friends."

"Will do, Boss," he said then made a face. "Listen, I need some help with all this paperwork and a field supervisor to keep things running smoothly, mostly so I can get a day off and more sleep at home instead of at the office."

"Promote from within—I think a couple of the retirees were field sergeants on LA, and let Linda hire you a full-time secretary. Each of those moves will require another hundred billable hours a week."

"I can't get out and sell with all this other crap on my plate," he said.

"You want me to hire a salesman?"

"This GM title comes with a lot of work, Rollo."

"I figure I just lightened your load by forty percent, costing us over a grand a week," I said. "And you're already making more than me."

"I do more," was his parting shot.

That afternoon, a call came in specifically asking for me by name, refusing to identify herself to Ruth. "This is Rollo. Can I help you?"

"You probably could have twenty-three years ago." Her southern drawl was distinct. "This is a voice from your past, sugar."

"Diana?" The hairs on the back of my neck were doing a jig.

"My, my, you *do* remember. I would've bet you forgot all about little ol' me, you being a big shot Hollywood private eye and all." Her accent was not hiding the intended sarcasm.

"Okay, I get it. You're still pissed because I left without saying goodbye. But that was sure a long time ago, so why the call all these years later?"

"I need to talk to you and can't discuss it on the phone. I need your help. Can we meet this afternoon?"

"I guess you're not in Atlanta, so where are you?

"Norwalk."

"Come to my office."

"Do I need an appointment?"

"Nope. I'm hoping I'll be glad to see you."

"Actually, I'm right downstairs in the coffee shop. I'll see you in two minutes," she said and ended the call.

My brain filled with fond memories of Georgia and a torrid affair with a Georgia Belle named Di near the end of my military commitment. Back then, my wild side persona was running at top speed, fueled by booze, sex, and rock 'n roll. Fun times, no responsibilities, a monthly paycheck, and guilt money from my dad made me a player. Freddie Fender's *Wasted Days and Wasted Nights* was my favorite song on the oldies station I rocked to back then. I left the army, Hardship Discharge in hand, and never looked back, fearing what I'd see.

*What did she mean by that snarky remark, "You sure could have twenty-three years ago," and what kind of help did she need?*

# CHAPTER 7

## REVELATIONS

**I ROSE FROM** my desk as Ruth showed the woman from my past into my office. Diana stood there motionless, just inside the door, her eyes appraising her surroundings before setting her gaze on me. I forced a smile and offered my hand. "Di," I said, "what a surprise."

She hesitated a few more heartbeats before stepping forward. "Roland," she said, giving my hand a little fingertip squeeze with her left before taking a seat. A hint of orange blossoms caught my attention, bringing back long-forgotten memories. Her smile lacked warmth, and her eyes were red-rimmed and lacked the sparkling flirty-ness I remembered. She had aged but still looked a decade younger than her forty-one years.

"Coffee?" I asked, stepping toward the credenza.

"No thanks. I drank two downstairs working up the nerve to call."

As she clutched her purse with both hands to quell their trembling, I noticed her wedding ring. "So, what's up, buttercup? How long have you been living in California?"

"I don't. I still live a bit outside of Augusta—bigger house, better neighborhood. But my married daughter lives in Norwalk. I'm just visiting. You calling me buttercup takes me back a ways," she said, her downcast eyes and solemn tone telling me whatever this was about wasn't good.

"I take it you're not here to talk about old times," I said, refilling my cup and sitting down. "How can I help you?"

"My daughter, Laura, is sick. She has a blood disorder called aplastic anemia and needs a bone marrow transplant. The doctors told us the best match comes from a parent or sibling. Her sister wasn't a good match because she had a different father than Laura, and my medical issues ruled me out. So that leaves her father." Tears welled up and began to flow as she took a handkerchief from her purse with shaking hands. Some contents spilled to the floor and I got up to help retrieve them.

"So, you don't know where he is and want me to find him?" I asked, handing her a lipstick and rental car keys.

"No, that's not why I'm here, Rollo," she said, surprising me as I returned to my seat. She took a deep breath and continued. "I came to beg for your help because… *you're* Laura's father, and she needs her father now!"

I sat in stunned silence. This gut punch from an old flame overwhelmed me with guilt and sadness. And

Diana piled on. She told her story of unwed motherhood, desperation, and struggle. A failed marriage that produced another child followed. But then her tone changed when telling me of the happiness that arrived in the form of a Mister Right named Clifford Wright. I smiled, hearing of his wholehearted embrace of Diana and her two daughters. They recently celebrated their eleventh wedding anniversary.

Then Di informed me I was now a grandfather. My new granddaughter, Leigh, was almost a year older than my youngest daughter. My mind was having a hard time assimilating all she was telling me. I raised my hands in surrender to make Diana stop talking while I caught my breath. I had many questions but settled on one. "When can I meet our daughter and grandchild?"

"Tomorrow?" And we set a time and place. We exchanged cell numbers, and I walked her to the elevator. The elevator's arrival broke up an awkward hug.

"Tomorrow then," I said. A goodbye didn't seem appropriate.

Emotionally wrung out, I returned to my office to regain some balance. If sixty minutes with Di kicked my ass, what would twenty-plus years have done, killed me? I reached into the bottom right desk drawer for a Jack Daniels bracer. Two large gulps tried to fight their way back up, but I toughed it out.

I started replaying today's scene in my head. She was not bitter about the mess a disappearing boyfriend left her to face alone. Why not seek me out? I remember she had an older sister, but Di didn't mention her or the parents she lived with at the time. How come? There'd be more conversations, I'm sure. But what about the daughter we conceived? And her illness. Then I realized I didn't know our daughter Laura's last name. *Well, dude, big surprises can cause brain farts.*

I gave Manny the address where I was to meet Laura and my grandchild tomorrow and asked him to search Norwalk property records then run the names attached to the location.

I fired up my computer and Googled *aplastic anemia.* It turns out to be a severe blood disorder, often fatal. The more I read, the more I feared for the daughter I'd never met. Another sip and I put Jack back in his drawer.

O   O   O

Linda's car was in the driveway when I arrived home, meaning my life wasn't entirely upside down, just sideways. Our giant cat of indeterminate age, El Gato, greeted me at the door, seemingly glad to see me. *Or maybe the aroma of fried chicken had him in a dither.*

"Honey, I'm home!" I announced, noticing the floral bouquet on the entry table. *Thank you, Ruth.*

"We're in the kitchen," Linda called out, the cheeriness in her voice giving me hope.

Marlowe bounced excitedly in her inflatable chair, extending her arms as I reached to pick her up and give her a smooch. Linda had her back to me, busily mashing potatoes. A spark of desire rushed through me as I admired the view. Thanks to our Peloton cycle, the weight gained during pregnancy was almost gone.

"How was your day?" she asked as I kissed the back of her neck, and Marlowe squirmed and giggled between us.

"Different," I said, and the debate in my head started again. Should I wait to tell Linda until after tomorrow's meeting with my new daughter? *"No guts, no glory,"* the ballsy me whispered. *"Is Linda ready for another helping of crap on her plate?"* The worrying me countered, "I'll tell you all about it after supper. I'm starving."

I waited until after we polished off the bottle of Chablis to give my report of the surprise visit of an old flame and the results produced by a torrid two-month affair. "OMG!" was Linda's response, followed by a heated grilling that left me skewered and seeking help from Jack Daniels. After wondering how many more children sired by me were still out there, she asked, "Why is it that men think birth control is only a woman's responsibility?"

I thought for a bit, sipped more Tennessee whiskey, and then said, "I haven't given it much thought. Maybe because men don't get pregnant?"

After an eye roll, she shocked me with: "I'd like to be with you when you meet your daughter and new granddaughter tomorrow, okay?" To her credit, she was concerned and wanted to know what she could do to help.

"Of course," I said. "That would be wonderful."

"I can't believe I'm married to someone's grandfather!"

# CHAPTER 8

## FAMILY MATTERS

**MY CADDY'S NAVIGATION** confirmed we were at our destination. I parked across the street, and we got out. Linda smoothed her skirt before walking around and taking hold of my arm to be led to the well-kept sizeable two-story home. The door opened as we approached the porch, and Diana stepped out to greet us.

"Diana, this is my wife, Linda," I said. "She wanted to meet everyone."

"Nice to meet you," Di said, awkward nods exchanged, and we entered the home. "Laura has fixed some lunch for us out on the patio." And she led us through the living room to the back of the house. Anticipation seized me as we walked onto the screened-in patio.

Laura looked up from the table and smiled. She looked frail, a sadness in her eyes that her smile could not hide. Yet, Laura bore an unmistakable resemblance to my other adult daughter, Melissa. "Welcome to our home," she said.

To her right, a baby sat in a playpen. The pink dress and matching hair ribbon had me conclude this was my granddaughter, Leigh. She was busy with a pacifier in her mouth and a plastic rattle in her hand. Linda went right to her.

"This beautiful baby must be Leigh," Linda said. "May I pick her up?"

"Sure. Mom says you have a seven-month-old daughter yourself," Laura said. And the ice was broken, as Di added another place setting for the surprise guest.

Small talk accompanied a lunch of petite egg salad sandwiches and lemonade. Linda went with Laura when it came time to change Leigh's Pampers, leaving Di and me alone.

"Convinced?" Di asked.

"She looks a lot like her sister Mel. Listen, Di, I never doubted what you told me, so where do we go from here?"

"I'll notify her doctor this afternoon and make an appointment for you at the hospital ASAP for all the tests you'll need to take."

My "I'll study hard for them" got me a smile, and then she teared up. I took her hand and told her I was glad she found me and would do whatever I could for our daughter.

The three girls returned, Laura now carrying my granddaughter, Leigh. She was smiling and walked straight to me. "Leigh, I want you to meet your grandfather, Roland Michaels," she said and handed her daughter to me. "What do you think, Dad?"

Leigh settled in my arms and stared into my eyes, touching my soul. "She's beautiful," was all I could muster.

o   o   o

On the drive back to Michaels & Associates, I told Linda of my conversation with Diana and the medical testing I'd soon be experiencing. We sensed my new daughter was on the clock, judging from her appearance and all that Di had said. Linda said her conversation with Laura was sobering when Laura confided a plan was in place for Di to raise the baby if Laura didn't pull through. Laura also told Linda that I was her best hope of recovery and that she and her mother prayed I was the answer God sent so Leigh would grow up with a mom.

My mother often said, "God works in mysterious ways." That I could be a *God-sent best hope* made me think He must have a backup plan.

As usual, Linda's response to all of this was terrific. She was my rock, the calm in the eye of the storm now swirling around me, but what she said next blew me away: "I'll stick it out at the company while we get through this as a family."

"I love you," was all I could say.

We then speculated on what kind of man my daughter had married. Laura told us her husband, Gary Franks, was in charge of West Coast sales for a big pharma company headquartered in Seattle. Their neighborhood and home said Gary made a lot of money. If money could make his wife well, Laura would be the picture of health right now. That I could be the answer to anyone's prayers was definitely something I wasn't used to.

Pandemic bullshit was negatively impacting business at Michaels & Associates. When we arrived, Ruth was masked with one of those masks that looked like a feedbag. She was the only one among us not vaxxed due to other health issues. Today, Ruth was running the joint single-handedly. Manny the Nerd, her usual partner, could do his job from anywhere in the world except where he was today: in court. He and his attorney, Art, were fighting a chicken shit battery arrest from almost a year ago. Being big and black attracted a particular element that thought they needed another notch on their "tough guy" belt. Choosing to call out Emanuel Hemmings usually resulted in the caller's trip to the ER. But that's another story.

Clancy, another partner, was running an employee theft case so we could make payroll. We hadn't had a walk-in for over two weeks. Things were slow with no accidents to investigate, no missing persons to find, and no backgrounds that needed searching. Only Jack's security gigs were keeping us above water.

Ruth handed me a message slip and said, "This might be something good. The caller says he was referred by Chief Gregory Allen, whoever that is."

"If it weren't for that ugly mask you're wearing, I'd give you a big kiss," I said, making Linda smile.

"I'd take it off if Linda wasn't here just to see if you're anywhere as good as you think you are!" Ruth answered, Linda snickered, and I retreated to my office. The name on the call slip said Ed Russell, but the area code was 213, the same as ours and two hundred miles from Chief Allen's beat. I called the chief first.

# CHAPTER 9

## A CASE

**GREG ALLEN WAS** my captain when I was medically pensioned off the LAPD eight years ago. We had bumped shoulders many times during my fifteen-year abbreviated law enforcement career. He once opined, "I thought you'd finish your twenty on the Rubber Gun Squad, Michaels." But we remained friends. He was now chief in a midsized town up north. I had his personal number on speed dial.

He answered in the middle of the third ring. "How's it hanging, Rollo?"

"I'm assuming you're alone and not on speakerphone, so I'll tell you. I stepped on it, again."

"Your Johnson must be looking like a platypus. What did you do this time?"

"Got arrested."

"Geez, Rollo! Now, what for?"

"Battery on a PO," I said and ran the five-minute version down to him. His questions added another five minutes to the conversation; before I could ask him about the client, he referred to Michaels & Associates.

"You must enjoy getting your ass kicked. I thought Roberts was better than that, and you smarter than that."

"It was an ambush," I said. We could have continued for another ten minutes before asking about the weather, but adding a paying client excited me more. "Tell me about your only other friend, Ed Russell."

"Ed is a partner in an LA law firm involved in a big malpractice suit involving hundreds of millions. He and his wife are also in the middle of a contentious divorce. Here's the thing, she had signed a prenup, and he suspects the wife of leaking case info to the other side for revenge and money."

"You know we don't do divorce work, and I'm not that fond of attorneys."

"Do me a favor and talk to Ed. By the way, isn't your partner, Art Salazar, one, and wasn't he your divorce lawyer?"

"When Marie's lawyer got done, I couldn't afford to pay Art. That's why we became partners."

I said goodbye and punched in the numbers for Ed Russell. A woman answered after the second ring. "Kaufman and Russell, how may we help you?" She didn't sound like a *we*.

"Roland Michaels here, returning Ed's call."

"*Mister* Russell is with a client right now. May we call you back?"

My "No, but Ed can," seemed to stump her for a few beats. "He has my number," I prompted.

"And so do I, Mr. Michaels," she said. And I could almost hear her grin.

I'd usually have Manny do a computer workup on a prospective client like the law firm Kaufman & Russell, and he'd have ten pages for me in less than ten minutes, telling me who, what, and some of the where and why of what I'd be dealing with but not today. Manny's rap sheet was probably why he and Art were in court today, his nine-year-old murder arrest and conviction being a big deal on anyone's rap sheet, a record that left out the pertinent part: Emanuel Hemmings served seven years in prison for a crime he didn't commit. That I was the one who found the real culprit played a big part in Manny coming to work for us. So was the $190K settlement Art got for him from the state of California.

Linda stuck her head in the door to announce my ex was on the phone wanting to know if I could talk. I picked up. "Hello, Marie. What's up?"

"Couple of things. First, my cousin Angela called from Long Island in tears. Says the Feds slapped a lean on her home with a notice to get out in ninety days or be removed. Can you believe it?"

"I'm not surprised," I said. "The RICO charges the Feds hung on Vinnie were draconian, specifically designed to put organized crime members out of business and confiscate ill-gotten gains. Angie should contact

Uncle Vinnie's lawyer. What about his bar and restaurant in Fort Salonga?"

"That's always belonged to Angie under her maiden name at least on paper. She said it was an engagement present he gave her, along with the ring."

"Smart. I didn't know that," I said.

"Listen, I really called to tell you a pair of detectives came by this morning to ask me about you and that bastard cop, Joe Roberts. They told me you put him in the hospital, so I said that had nothing to do with me, but Roberts probably had it coming. I kind of enjoyed watching you all over the TV news."

"Roberts wants to pin your boyfriend's murder on me," I said.

"There's something you should know, Rollo. I never shot Ernie—our son did. Brandon heard the fight and came running down the hall with my gun. Seeing me on the bloody floor and Ernie running out the door, Brandon fired twice to make sure the bastard kept on running. We made up the story that I fired the gun in self-defense, but we were stuck with it when the officers found the blood outside."

I was stunned. They cooked up a story that only made it worse for everybody. I was pissed that my son hadn't confided in me. But then another thought took shape in my brain. After ten seconds of silence, I hit her with a "Hello! Who have you told about your case?"

"Only my cousin, Angie, but she'd never tell anybody."

"Not even her husband?"

"Oh, no…you think Uncle Vin…oh my god, Rollo?" It wasn't a stretch to conclude that Big Vinnie, even from his prison cell, could've sicced his best Button Man, Soldier Boy Mahan, on anyone threatening a family member.

"You might ask your cousin. She'd know, for sure. Just not on her phone." Shouts and cheers in the outer office interrupted. "I've got to go, Marie," I said.

Art burst into my office. "Case dismissed," he yelled.

"You're on a roll, Pard. First, Marie, then me, and now, Manny. It's about time for a paying gig."

"You're not out of the woods yet. The city needs your ass convicted, so they don't get sued," he said, his big smile beaming. "You know, if we sued everybody kicking your ass, I wouldn't have time for your family and friends' cases." We slapped high-fives as he took a seat. "We need to expunge Manny's arrest record. Each time he bumps into the law, the cops run his record, and boom! They want to book his ass."

"That would definitely lighten your case load, Counselor. I'm glad you're back. I got a possible case I might need to bring you in on. Kaufman & Russell ring any bells for you?"

"Sure, a big LA law firm taking up two floors of a Spring Street high-rise. Why do you ask?"

I filled him in, and he agreed to listen in on Ed's call when it came. He cautioned they had several in-house investigators and expressed his skepticism about why us.

An hour later, Ed Russell called and wished to meet at a neutral site. Ed suggested a quiet booth at Musso & Frank's might be convenient. After shooting down my request to bring along my partner, we settled on five o'clock.

I told Art the guy might be a control freak. He said Russell's problem might be a personal one. "Probably wishes to keep it out of his office and away from his partners, divorce crap, and all. Be careful."

Linda had left two hours ago to relieve Maricela, our cleaning lady and part-time babysitter, leaving me with the company loaner we used for surveillance and tailing. Nondescript, it sure wouldn't impress a big-time attorney of Ed's ilk nor the illegal alien parking valet supporting a family with minimum wages and the many unreported $5 tips that doubled his income.

Henry, the maître d', said Mr. Russell had called, reserving a table but wasn't here yet. I followed him to a booth close to the kitchen. Cooking smells and snippets of Spanish slipped out every time the door swung open. Although tequila crossed my mind, I asked Henry for a double Jack on the rocks to be sociable. Two sips later, Henry escorted a man in a tailored suit costing a thousand dollars more than anything in my closet to the booth. I stood as he offered his hand and introduced himself.

That out of the way, we slid into the booth. He ordered a single-malt scotch-on-the-rocks I'd never heard of and asked, "Where do you live, Rollo?" which struck me as odd.

"The Valley."

"You don't sound like a Valley guy."

"Nor a Valley *girl*," I said. "New York, born and raised. But I'm sure you know all about me, or we wouldn't be here. How can Michaels & Associates be of help to you?"

"You cut right to the chase. I like that." He then told me a love story of a guy in his early fifties falling for a twenty-something employee. A year of flowers, candy, and many romantic getaway weekends, had them tie the knot. After five years of marital bliss, maybe less, a young studly leads the wife astray. LA being a showbiz town in the middle of the electronic age and the miracle of the iPhone, she discovers Studly has been secretly recording their lovemaking. The wife breaks off the affair and confesses all to her husband. After much brooding, they agree to marriage counseling, kiss, and make up. "After all," Ed explained, "who hasn't strayed?" This comment makes me wonder how deep a background check he had done on me.

Turns out, the spurned studly, Sean Cooper, wasn't done with Candace Russell quite yet. He needed the costar of his porn flick for a few more close-ups. He sent Candy a movie trailer of select action scenes to elicit her return to the set. The implied threat of a public release was an attention-getter. To not be a complete jerk about it, he said he might settle for financial restitution for all the hard work he invested in the project.

Ed ponied up ten grand to protect his wife's reputation, if not her virtue. That was three months ago. A second request came a month after the first, but this time Studly called the payment a loan. He claimed he was strapped for cash and needed to pay off his investors after folding his and Candy's film project. Again, Ed paid. But when the third request came three weeks later via a text message, Ed texted back, *"No mas!"* Later that night, Ed received three still photos on his phone, showing his wife in a most compromising position. Hurt and anger-filled, he went to Candy and showed her the pictures on his phone. Not surprisingly, she had received the same three on her cell from Studly's number and no text.

The following morning they went to Studly's WeHo apartment to confront him. They found the police had barricaded the door with a crisscross of yellow CRIME SCENE tape. They checked with the building manager, who said Sean Cooper had been stabbed to death in his apartment a week ago.

I watched Ed's hands tremble as he stared into his Scotch. "Problem solved, no?" I asked.

"No, damn it. Don't you see? Someone has Cooper's phone days after his murder. We're screwed."

"Not if you go to the police."

"Yeah, right. Then we become suspects, press leaks expose my firm to bad publicity and embarrassment, and clients jump ship. We have active cases that could net us tens of millions. There has to be another way."

"I gave you the best option, Counselor. Give the cops your phones, texts, and photos. You'd be surprised what they can do with the info."

"We deleted all of it when we found out about the murder. Last night Candace got a one-word text from an unknown caller. 'Pictures' was all it said."

"How much do you guys charge clients for investigator time?"

"gator time?"

"Hundred an hour."

"And the hourly rate for legal work?"

"Three to five." He wiped the sweat from his forehead and called a waiter over. "Another round, here, please."

"Make mine coffee," I said. "I'll need to interview your wife in the morning."

"Why?"

"See if I want to take the case."

"I was told you were dealing with a similar situation involving your ex-wife."

"News travels. Boyfriend murders trending in cyberspace? Yes, my ex-wife's boyfriend was murdered, and it could cause a distraction for me working for you and your wife. But, unlike you, I have a good lawyer."

'Touché, Michaels." A slight flush of anger crossed his face. He went on to say he'd bring his wife to Michaels & Associates tomorrow at ten. Telling him I'd prefer to meet with her alone ruffled his feathers even more, but he agreed to wait in the coffee shop downstairs. We said our goodbyes and left, freeing up the table no Musso & Frank's regular would want or ever be offered.

I figured I'd take the case as long as Art kept me out of jail or Candace Russell told me something that was a deal breaker tomorrow at ten.

# CHAPTER 10

## THE WIFE

**NEXT MORNING, CANDACE** Russell called to say she'd be late and her husband wouldn't be coming. We rescheduled for 11:00, giving me enough time to fill Art in. He advised me to strongly urge her to go to the police before signing her up, pointing out all the trouble we would be opening ourselves up to by withholding evidence in a homicide case.

"You're already on your alma mater's shit list," he said. "Why poke the bear?"

Linda entered my office wearing one of those ugly N95 masks from Sam's Club. Art and I weren't masked up, but Ruth and Manny were. I hadn't seen Clancy this morning but knew Linda wanted everyone who entered wearing a mask. The "MASK REQUIRED" sign hung on the door to our suite whenever she brought our daughter to the office. We've been using our conference room as a daycare nursery for Marlowe for over three months now. The upsurge of another Covid variant had Linda worried. Since we were expecting visitors today, and you never know where anyone who enters has been or who they stood next to in the elevator, she insisted we mask. Art's hung under his chin, and mine sat within arm's reach on my desk.

"Diana called and says she got you an appointment at the hospital tomorrow morning at eight for the pre-op physical, testing, and interview. Di and Laura will be there to introduce you to Laura's doctors. No food or liquids after midnight for blood testing and whatever," Linda said and hurried out as if Art and I were lepers.

Art did a double take and asked, "What's going on, Pard?"

So I told him of the daughter I never knew about until two days ago and the woman who gave birth to her who I *knew* over twenty years ago. Then I explained Laura's medical situation and need for a bone marrow transplant from her biological father, who she met for the first time yesterday.

The telling and explaining to the lawyerly Art ended when Ruth announced the arrival of Mrs. Russell on the intercom. "Show her in, please," I said. The door opened, and we stood to greet our prospective client.

"Mrs. Russell, I'm Roland Michaels," I said, offering her my hand, but she opted for three fingertips. "And this is my partner, Arturo Salazar. Please have a seat. You may remove your mask if you'd be more comfortable."

Dressed to impress, she removed her cloth mask and smiled. Tall and lithe, she gracefully took the seat offered. It was easy to see why her husband was attracted to her. Long blond tresses flowed to her shoulders, and just the right amount of luminous liner accented her blue-gray eyes. Her bright red lip gloss appeared freshly applied.

"May I offer you some coffee?" It took her a few heartbeats to respond, ignoring Art while taking my measure.

"No, thank you, Mr. Michaels. My husband said you wanted to talk to me before you decided to take our case?"

"Yes. I wanted to hear your take on all that occurred between you and Sean Cooper after breaking off the affair."

She winced like I had slapped her in the face. Tears welled in her eyes. I wondered how she'd hold up when somebody like a Joe Roberts sat her down in a police interrogation room. Her reaction made me feel like an ass. Art gave me an almost imperceptible head shake and slid our standby Kleenex box across the desk to her. She popped one out and dabbed a tear, careful not to smear her makeup. "We were lovers, and I thought he was as serious as I was. I told him I would leave my husband."

I nodded, but she didn't continue. "So tell us, how did you and Sean meet?"

"He was my fitness trainer at the gym I belonged to in West Hollywood. One-hour sessions twice a week for over a year."

"Still a member?" Art asked.

"No. I stopped when I discovered he was recording me—us."

After we got all the whens, wheres, and whys throughout the affair answered to Art's satisfaction, I got down to the nitty-gritty. "Do you think your husband killed Sean?" Her answer wasn't an immediate response, giving me some new doubts and raised Art's eyebrows.

"No," she finally said. "If my husband was a violent man, why not kill me? He was as surprised as I was when the manager told us Sean was dead, murdered."

Art and I saw nothing wrong with her answer. "Did *you* kill Sean?" was my follow-up.

This time her "No" was unencumbered by thought.

"Okay. We'll take your case if you and your husband agree to hire Art as your attorney," I said. Confusion was written all over her face, so I added, "Art will explain it to your husband if he can get in to see you and Ed later today. We'll need paperwork signed and a $10,000 retainer to get started."

Agreeing, she stood, and we shook hands. I walked Candace Russell to the elevator after validating her parking stub. I was pretty sure her "Thank you" was for taking the case to retrieve the compromising images Sean Cooper had recorded and not for validating her parking stub.

Art made the appointment with Ed Russell by calling my new friend, Russell's private secretary, Ms. Shaw. Telling her Mr. Michaels asked him to call got him through to Ed Russell. They agreed to a five o'clock meeting.

I got together with Manny to see what he could do for us in cyberspace with Sean Cooper's name. He was back in ten minutes to tell me Cooper didn't appear to exist until four years ago when he opened a Facebook account.

We all took an early out and closed shop at 4:30.

Later that night, Art called me at home. "Russell put me through a vigorous *voir dire* before signing on the dotted line. I again told him and his wife of the hazards of holding back information from the authorities. He told me they would remain mute and that you and I are restricted by law from divulging anything he or his wife tells us like I was a first-year law student. My impression? A little pompous, but he wouldn't fold under pressure. How's your buddy, the chief, connected to this guy?"

"I don't know. Did you ask?"

"No. Was I supposed to?"

# CHAPTER 11

## MEDICAL

*I TOOK A* couple of deep breaths before I masked to enter the hospital. Once inside, a screener at the door took my temperature without a thermometer and asked the reason for my visit. My "tests" response had her direct me to a check-in line where I took a number and waited to be called. I wondered why we did the number thing since we were standing in a line. Wouldn't calling out "Next" serve the purpose? Three young ladies sat behind windowed computer stations and took turns calling numbers. After about four minutes, I went from fifth to next in line.

"Twenty-seven," the redhead yelled. I looked at my ticket. It said 29. *WT…?* A woman hurried to the redhead's window, the blond woman in the next window called "28," and another woman came around me in a wheelchair shouting "Here!" The lady in the third window then called "30." The guy behind me stepped around and headed to the third window. On the verge of blowing a fuse, I started to worry about my new daughter's well-being in this joint, but the redhead called my number.

After entering my name, DOB, vax dates, and insurance cards into their system, she directed me to Dr. Rachael Martin's office on the third floor. My masked daughter and Di greeted me with hugs when I entered five minutes late.

"We were getting nervous, Dad," Laura said. I couldn't help but notice the dark circles around her eyes and the paleness of her face, sans makeup. Di's brow was wrinkled with concern.

"Sorry, delayed at the check-in station."

A door opened, and a nurse handed me a clipboard with a lot of paperwork I needed to fill out. I sat between mother and daughter and got to it as they looked on. Medical history included gunshot and other wounds, broken bones, surgeries, diseases checked off, and approximate dates guessed. A list of meds and supplements and drug and alcohol use questions made the girls uncomfortable, but I saw them peeking at my answers. I finished with the paperwork and was now ready to bleed, pee in a jar, get x-rays, and whatever else the doc needed before the consult. My girls left for the café downstairs as the nurse took me away.

An hour later, we met with Laura's doctor. Rachael Martin was about my age, dressed in business attire, a white blouse, blue skirt, and matching jacket. Her dark brown hair streaked with gold highlights was held back behind her ears with black-rimmed glasses and a jeweled lanyard. Her green eyes gave me what I took to be her stern look, her white surgical mask making her hard to read.

"It says here you've had two hip replacement surgeries, Mr. Michaels. I don't see how we can extract bone marrow from artificial hip bones." Laura burst into tears, and Di gasped.

"Only my left hip, Doctor. We replaced the twelve-year-old model about a year ago with a new and improved one. My right hip is all me. I understand that you can harvest marrow from my tibia, also."

"True. You recently suffered a rib injury?"

"My doctor says I'm healing nicely."

"Do your bones break easily, Mr. Michaels?"

"No, Dr. Martin. My hip was broken by a high-speed car with a drug-addled driver behind the wheel. My two ribs were chipped by a bullet the first time, then broken by an overzealous FBI agent the next time, and broken again in a recent altercation. Same ribs all three times," I said.

My new family members seemed shocked. The doctor reddened and blinked a couple of times then said, "You know we might have to do this procedure more than once?"

"Whatever it takes, Doctor."

Addressing us all, she said, "Since time is of the essence, can we do this next Tuesday, depending on your DNA analysis, the results of which we'll have Monday?"

"Yes!" Diana shouted, and I nodded. Laura just cried. The good doctor turned us over to an assistant with more questions requiring another hour to answer, consent forms signed, lists of dos and don'ts handed out, and we were done.

My Tuesday check-in time was 7:00 a.m. for Laura's 1:00 p.m. infusion procedure. But my daughter could be hospitalized for as long as three weeks, starting tomorrow. The round of chemo, followed by radiation to suppress her immune system, sounded terrible. Hugs were exchanged in the parking lot before going our separate ways, the new ladies in my life to Norwalk, me to Wilshire Boulevard where duty called.

# CHAPTER 12

## CASE STRATEGY

**ART GREETED ME** with the news Ed Russell's retainer check had cleared the bank. His team strategy in the case was to have me call my buddy, Detective Dan "Tank" Tankersley of Sheriff's Homicide Bureau, to see what I might find out about the Sean Cooper murder. He also assigned Manny to further search cyberspace for anything connected with Cooper.

We started with the assumption Candace Russell wasn't Cooper's only shakedown victim. Then there were the photos and texts from Cooper's phone, miraculously sent three days AD. Call history could lead us to the killer, who might be a partner, another victim, or a Cooper acquaintance. We'd be stuck with four million suspects if it was a random killer off the streets. Art and

I agreed it was a good bet Cooper's killer had the phone. We wondered if the sheriffs found any other electronics in the apartment.

So far, all we had was Cooper's currently turned-off phone number, thanks to Hollywood electronic surveillance expert and friend, Peter Gunn. But Gunn could nail down the cell tower used for the two texts and photos sent to our clients yesterday. Sometimes, who you know is worth as much as what you know in this business.

I called Detective Tankersley on his cell, not wanting to go through all the screening that calling his workplace would produce.

"I must've been drunk or hungover when I gave you my cell number, Michaels."

"Neither one, Danny Boy. I got it off a shithouse wall."

"You calling to ruin the rest of my day?"

"Who is working the Sean Cooper murder?"

After a five-count, he asked, "Why?"

"I might be able to shed some light if someone is in a trading mood."

"What you got?"

"My client was dating him for a time about a year ago, then broke it off. Four days ago, she got a text from him, wanting money."

"We're a week in with very little to share. One thing I know for sure, your client didn't get a text from Sean Cooper. Prints say his real name is Cooper Paul Henderson, aka Paul Cooper, Paul Henderson, a twenty-nine-year-old with a DOB of 6-26-93. Male Caucasian, six-one, 180, brown and blue, tats both arms, torso scar left side. The coroner says the cause of death was a fragmented .22 caliber slug that rattled around, mushing his brain. No known next of kin. He has a couple of felony arrests for grand theft and a petty theft with a prior when stealing was still a crime. He had one outstanding traffic warrant that'll never get paid for driving without a license. What's the cell number he called your client on? I'll get his call history."

"Sorry, Tank, the client wouldn't give it to me. Were any electronics found at the scene?"

"Nope. We figured it was a residential robbery gone bad." His follow-up, "Give me your client's name and number. I'll call her and get it myself, asshole," was said without levity.

"I can't, Tank. Her lawyer's the one who hired me, the attorney-client privilege thing. I will get you the phone number, though."

"Well, what the fuck do you have for me?"

"He was blackmailing her with many compromising videos of him and her getting it on. I think that was his scam, blackmailing married women. My client suspected he had other ladies on the string. The text by the unknown person wanted more money from her and her husband. Thinking it was Cooper, they went to his apartment to reason with him and buy the video for ten thou. They get there, and your yellow Crime Scene tape leads to conversations with a nosey neighbor and the manager, then they beat feet. That was Friday."

"Probably the same neighbor who told us about a number of unknown women looking for the guy. Get me the number and the attorney's name, or I'll squeeze your balls until you go blind."

"Ouch! That's just mean. Did you find any other electronics in his apartment, like computers, burner phones, video cameras?"

"Asked and answered. Only phone jacks and USB cables were left behind. Names and numbers might get you something." *Click!* And he was gone, making me think no, or else why would they think "residential burglary gone wrong"?

I still felt bad about lying to a friend and brother of the badge. Rationalizing about kids wanting to go to college, a fat monthly alimony payment, and employees needing paychecks that didn't bounce didn't make it hurt any less. I'd stall Tank until tomorrow.

When I arrived at the office, the two donuts I scarfed down with coffee didn't do much to relieve my hunger. I gave Manny the additional info Tank supplied and headed to the little café downstairs. I ordered a Deluxe Club of bacon, ham, and cheese, a side of potato salad, and a chocolate malt.

Halfway through my meal, my cell gave me instant *agita*. It was my ex. "Yes, Marie, what's up?"

"That bastard detective was here again. This time saying he wanted to apologize for filing charges against me, adding that he knew all the stress it had caused for the family. He wanted to talk to Brandon about who he thought murdered you know who. I told him to fuck off before I broke his other arm." I heard a sense of pride in her voice.

"Good for you. Where's our son now?" I asked.

"With his friends, surfing at Zuma Beach."

"Tell him to stop by my place tonight for a fatherly talk."

"Okay. What are you going to tell him?"

"Man stuff." I then called Captain Malinka, Detective Roberts's boss.

Two minutes on hold, then "Hello, Rollo. You calling to confess your sins?"

"Last time I looked, you weren't a priest."

"I could take that a number of ways."

"Any way you like, Corrie. I thought Roberts was going to be off a few weeks."

"True. He's due back Monday after next. Why?"

"He was at my ex-wife's house looking for my son. You better put a GPS tracker on the SOB and keep him away from my family. He's off the rails, and the next time he starts sniffing around my family, I'll kick his ass."

"Hey, calm down, Rollo. Stay cool. I'll look into it. Just don't overload your ass talking shit to me. How's baby Marlowe?"

"More beautiful every day."

"Don't get caught up in some bullshit that could take you away from her."

"I hear you. He can come after me all he wants, but nobody screws with my family," I said and ended the call. No longer hungry, I forced down the last of the shake. Brain freeze competed with my upset stomach for my attention as I put my food in a go-box and returned to the office.

Manny followed me to my desk, dumped a load of printouts, and sat. "Guy's a player, boss. He has Facebook accounts under all the names you gave me and a couple more. He also is running a porn dot com with a bunch of bitches doin' him and him doin' them. None of his friends appear on more than one of his six Facebook accounts. I didn't try Twitter, Instagram, or Tiktok but he's probably on all of it. Which means he needed help to keep track of it all. He's even got a dating service with over a thousand registered users. I haven't done any name searches on it yet."

"Holy shit, this is huge. Get Art in here."

I filled Art in on my conversation with Tankersley and Manny's follow-up on what Tank gave me. When I got to the part where I promised to divulge the client's name and phone number, he became apoplectic and chastised me by threatening all my orifices.

"Hell, Pard, we have to give him something," I said.

"Give him some of the stuff Manny came up with, which should tie them up for a few days," Art said and then asked, "Can they find our client in any of that stuff?"

"Sure, depending on how good they are and how deep they want to dig," Manny said.

"I'll call tomorrow and give him the Facebook stuff and the dating site. It should keep them busy and off my back a few more days while we stay out front of them," I said.

Manny opined, "Give 'em the porn stuff that'll keep 'em busy for a week." He was getting cop humor by osmosis.

"Can you clone his Facebook sites, especially the one our client is a friend on?" I asked Manny.

"Will do. There's been *post mortem* traffic on three of Cooper's Facebook pages, including that one," he said and returned to his computer.

Then I told Art about Detective Roberts going to my ex-wife's house looking for my son this afternoon. That set Art on a mission to light a fire under the deputy DA's ass. That and my call to Captain Malinka should keep Roberts out of my hair for a while.

# CHAPTER 13

## MOUNTING PRESSURE

**HOMICIDE DICKS ARE** a special breed in any large police department. Highly skilled, intuitive, and relentless, they can sift through a pile of shit and ferret out the tiniest clues to make or break a case. None are afraid to get their hands dirty looking for a perp, regardless of whose toes get stepped on. Their fraternity is tight-knit, and an attack on one is a slight to all.

My breaking Joe Roberts's arm pissed off a bunch of LAPD's finest. Not just murder cops, but apparently motor cops, too. As I pulled into my driveway that evening, a motor cop pulled onto the sidewalk directly behind me, dropped his kickstand down, and dismounted his BMW motorcycle. As I stepped from my Escalade, he said, "License, registration, and proof of insurance, please."

"What's this about, Officer?" I said, reaching for my wallet as a four-door sedan grabbed the curb across from us. Being a keen observer, I made the occupants as a couple of plainclothes detectives.

"You failed to signal your turn into the driveway. You live here?"

I handed him my license and retired LAPD identification. Reading his name tag, I asked, "Tell me, Gomez, those two assholes across the street put you up to this?"

"I don't see any assholes across the street," he responded.

I reached for my cell, and he reached for his gun, dropping my IDs on the sidewalk. "You shitting me or what?" I pointed out the security camera hanging from the corner of my garage and held up my phone. "Smile for the camera, Officer. If you still want to see my registration and proof of insurance, call a supervisor." I flipped the bird to the plainclothes unit as they pulled from the curb, smiling and waving for my cell's camera.

To the motor cop's credit, he retrieved my ID from the sidewalk and handed it to me. "I don't know what I got caught up in here. Care to tell me?"

"I put a hurt on one of their buddies. In fact, I broke his arm."

"You're the guy in the video from the courthouse parking lot," he said, a light of recognition going on. "They told me you were ex-PD gone rogue."

"Couple of our 'brothers in blue' broke two of my ribs that day, had me pissing blood for a week, but it was worth it. Listen, Gomez, inform your sergeant how this went down," I said and gave him a business card. "He can call me if he needs to."

○　○　○

As often happens, my son showed up at dinnertime—not a problem for the love of my life. While Brandon entertained his sister Marlowe, Linda happily put another handful of frozen crinkle cuts in the air fryer, another six-ounce burger on the George Foreman grill and sliced up more lettuce, tomato, and onion. Voila! Her "beer or lemonade?" was our signal to gather around the table.

"Catch any killer waves, or was it all about girls in bikinis?" I asked, unable to tell if he was sunburned or embarrassed.

"I can surf the waves and check out bathing suits at the same time, Dad," he said, his smile always disarming.

Linda choked on her lemonade as my chest swelled with pride. She nailed me with, "Unlike your father, Brandon. He has to spit out his gum to tie his shoes." Her high-fiving Brandon made me smile.

It went on like that for twenty minutes. And dinner was done. Brandon and I teamed up to do the dishes, while Linda took Marlowe for a bath. After drying the dishes, my son and I went outside and sat by the pool.

Perceptive, he started the conversation with, "Mom told me Detective Roberts came to the house wanting to talk to me about who killed the asshole."

"Son, I want to make you aware of a few things. First, I don't want you talking to the police about anything without me or our lawyer, Art, being there with you. Got it?" He nodded.

"Secondly, if he just wanted to talk to you, he would've called Art or me. He's just trying to intimidate you and your mother." His head was bobbing up and down in cadence with each punctuation mark.

"Lastly," I said, making his eyebrows come together in concentration, "don't ever conspire with your mother to conceal facts from me again." He teared up, but I continued, "We would have come up with a better story of what happened that night. The truth would've had you get a slap on the wrist."

"I'm sorry, Dad. Mom made me promise."

"I know, son, and she knows that was wrong, and she's sorry, too. But I'm also proud you came to your mother's rescue." I took him in my arms to comfort us both. If Brandon's godfather, Vinnie, had the asshole killed, seemed like justice enough to me. But because of personal animosity, Joe Roberts would never let it go.

# CHAPTER 14

## BULL

**THE FOLLOWING DAY,** I called Tankersley on his cell and told him to expect an email from Michaels & Associates with a batch of attachments. Hoping to brighten his day, I emphasized our desire to cooperate with law enforcement and, when possible, fully.

He said, "Bullshit. I need your client's name and number to get my captain off my back. I don't suppose it's in the email."

"Attorney says no, Tank, but your IT people might be able to ferret it out from what I'm sending you. You can thank me later."

That out of the way, my Donut Jones had me balancing a couple of maple glazed on a full coffee mug and heading to Art's office. As I reached to place my midmorning feeding on the corner of his desk, Ruth announced, *"Pete Gunn on line two for Rollo,"* on the intercom. Art put him on speaker.

"Morning, Pete," I said. "What's up?"

"That phone was active for twenty minutes, around nine this morning. Sent a text to the same two numbers as last time, and five minutes later, received an eight-minute voice call from an 818 cell, probably a burner."

"Location?"

"Started out at the same tower on the West Side. The voice call was mobile, bouncing off towers in Sepulveda Pass and one on Mulholland. Went dark right at 9:15." He then gave me the two numbers called. I recognized both.

"Thanks, Pete. Keep us posted. You got my cell, right?"

"You kidding? I have everybody's. Later."

Art hung up his desk phone and asked, "How are you going to go at this now?"

I took a bite out of my donuts to think about it. I wound up eating both of them and drinking half the coffee while thinking through the options. "First, I want to know why we haven't heard from either Russell about the text Pete says was sent to the missus almost two hours ago. As for moving the case forward, the most direct approach would be to call the bad guys, set up a buy sting, rain down the wrath of the porn gods upon the sellers, and squeeze the shit out of them. The trouble is, our clients don't want their plight known by the public, possibly exposing Mrs. Russell's ass all over the World Wide Web. If we move, it could get nasty, maybe have to kill the asshole or get hurt trying."

"A guy like Russell would probably sue our asses, too," Art said, and he should know.

"I think I'll drop in at Kaufman & Russell unannounced, see what excuse they give for not notifying us about the latest texts."

"Maybe Candace has her phone shut off," Art said.

"With somebody threatening to ruin her reputation, I can't see her shutting off her cell. Probably sleeps with it these days."

"She's most likely scared shitless that Hubby sees her enjoy getting it on with Cooper."

O   O   O

Again, I was underdressed for this den of the self-important. Even the receptionist wore a tie and jacket, perfectly matching her blouse and skirt. She gave me a quick once-over with a tight smile and asked, "May I help you, sir?"

"Please tell Mr. Russell's secretary Roland Michaels is here to see Ed."

She relayed the message via her phone and said, "Yes," a couple of times with appropriate nods for emphasis then told me, "Ms. Shaw will be right with you."

"That's okay. I see her down there to the right," I said, causing the receptionist's jaw to drop as I headed down the hallway. Ms. Shaw was checking herself out in a wall mirror, adjusting her skirt. "You told me you have my number, but you never call." Her checks reddened a bit, but she held it together with a laugh.

"What brings you here today, Mr. Michaels?"

"Something's come up that I need to whisper in Ed's ear."

"He's with one of the partners, discussing a case. He instructed me to hold all calls. It shouldn't be too much longer, though. Come, sit with me at my desk and tell me all about your cops and robbers days. Didn't I see something about you getting arrested outside a courthouse? I didn't put it together the first time you were here."

I found that interesting. It meant she had cause to check me out, maybe Googled me. "Is that why you said you had my number the first time I called?"

Before she could answer, the door to the inner sanctum opened, and Ed Russell walked out talking with another lawyerly type, clamming up when he spotted me. A pat on the back had his visitor continue down the hall. Ed turned to me, "Michaels," he said with a smile and nod. "Are you here to see me or hit on my secretary?"

"Business before pleasure, Counselor." His smile grew more prominent as he waved me into his office. We sat in the appropriate places, surrounded by windows with views of downtown LA's high-rise history.

"I assume you have something for me that you couldn't convey in a phone call."

"I have some questions, a few concerns, and a brief status report. I wanted to do this in person to better gauge your reactions." I paused to let him voice any objections. None, so I continued. "We've been in contact with the Sheriff's Homicide Bureau and provided information our IT people discovered about Cooper."

"I thought I made it clear, no police." He wasn't happy with that, so I explained the whys and what fors, including the possibility of a large-scale criminal scheme involving more players than just Cooper and Russell's wife. I noted his reaction went back and forth between anger and fear. To his credit, he expressed sympathy for Mrs. Russell but none for himself. After answering his questions, I switched to asking mine.

"When did you first suspect your wife was having an affair?"

"I didn't!" Exclaiming righteous indignation while glancing at the wall clock and straightening up the pen in his inkwell, set off my bullshit alarm. I saved it for later.

"Did she suspect you had also strayed from the nest?"

"Is that what she told you?" It was a dodge. "Why are you going down this path? It's not why we hired you."

"Ed, when the homicide detectives link Candace to their victim, and they will, sooner or later, this is the path they'll go down. Right now, I'm a couple of steps ahead of them. If I can hand them Cooper's killer, they'll stop digging. But I can't stay out front of this unless you and your wife are upfront with me. Did Candace inform you of the text message she got from Cooper's phone this morning?"

"Hell no. Why did she tell you and not me? What did it say?" His shocked expression was consistent with what he said.

"That's just it, Ed, I don't know—she didn't call me about it, either. We are monitoring Cooper's phone whenever it goes live."

He picked up his desk phone and punched in two digits. A look of surprise crossed his face. "Hi, Patty.

Where's my wife?" There was a pause then, "Where did she say she was going or say when she'd be back?" He shook his head and ended the call by, slamming the phone. "Shit!"

"Problem?" I asked.

"She left over an hour ago, told Patty she had to meet someone." He took out his cell and called his wife. She didn't or wouldn't answer, so he left a voice message, "Where are you? Call me." He then opened a locater app. "She's in Santa Monica at a mall on Third Street."

When my cell vibrated, I stood and moved away from Ed. The screen said, "Pete Gunn." "What's up?" I asked.

"We're live in Santa Monica, so is one of your client's phones," Pete said.

"I know. The client is close by on Third Street."

"Oops, just went dead. This a meet?"

"Sure looks like it. Thanks, Bubba." I put my phone away and told Ed, "Your wife is meeting with the text messenger."

"How —"

"Phones. I wonder why she'd feel safe going alone to meet with a possible killer. I hope she didn't bring any cash payoff with her."

"Why not get it over with so we can go on with our lives?"

*Really? You that stupid, Ed?* I thought then explained the facts of life and death and my plan to *get it over with so we can go on with our lives.* We arranged to have a conference call when Candace returned, him and her, Art and me. Before I left, Ed rechecked his locator app. Her phone was now off, and he wasn't happy. Ed's next move proved he had severe trust issues when he checked his wife's car location with a Lojack app. It was not moving, showing it was still on Third.

# CHAPTER 15

## MISSING

**_I WANTED TO_** hightail it to Santa Monica, but reason told me I'd be wasting time looking for Candace Russell in a mall of twenty-plus shops and thousands of women. I was stumped why she would go to deal with a blackmailer and a possible murderer. And why was getting info out of her husband such an ordeal?

When I reached Wilshire and La Brea, it was past 3:30, and some idiot had parked in my spot. Clancy's slot was vacant, three places down, slightly easing my anger. The government plates were a further insult. I thought of letting the air out a couple of tires when an authoritative female voice shouted, "Hey, Michaels!"

Recognizing the voice, I said, "Be right with you, Cap, after I put holes in a couple of tires here."

"You do, and I'll bust a cap in your ass," Corrie Malinka said. "You want a cup of coffee, instead?"

"Always," I said. "I'm betting this has something to do with our mutual acquaintance, Joe Roberts?"

"How are your ribs, Rollo?" she said, rubbing it in as we walked up the ramp to the street level and the coffee shop. I just shook my head and held the door for her. "What? I can't come by to see how you're healing?"

We ordered two double-shots at the counter, and Malinka paid with a ten-spot. "Keep the change." We took the farthest table while our smiling Barista, Ernesto, worked the hissing espresso machine.

"So, who sent you?"

"Bureau chief wants to know how far you want to go with this Joe Roberts thing."

"My lawyer says his cut of six figures might also be six figures and cautioned me not to talk to any LAPD representatives, no matter how friendly they act or good-looking they may be."

"This isn't an act, Rollo. I am a friend. What do you want me to tell my chief?" Before I answered, Ernesto showed up with our coffees. I put two packets of raw sugar in mine, Malinka opting for just one.

"Tell him what I just said about the numbers. We're coming down on the city for malicious prosecution, false arrest, bodily injury, and police harassment. You can add my lawyer said the city attorney is out there throwing money at BLM and Antifa rioters, and the like. I also think my hip replacement is acting up." I faked a grimace for emphasis.

"I sent Lt. Dacey to Roberts's house to order him to stay away from you and your family. Internal Affairs is handling your complaint," she said.

"The last two who came to see me implied the department would circle the wagons and pursue the battery on Roberts. I was inclined to cut Joe some slack, but then he shows up harassing my ex and threatening my son. My lawyer's pretty sure we can win this pissing contest." My espresso was sweet and still warm when I knocked it back. Corrie took a sip and made a face. "You need more sugar."

"No, I'm sweet enough," she said. *I always suspected that but never found out for sure.*

I filled Art in at the office on how my afternoon had gone. While I was most concerned about our Russell clients, he was most interested in my meeting with Captain Malinka. It was all about the dollar amount for him, probably because the name on the door wasn't Salazar & Associates. He insisted I write up my meeting with Malinka, word for word. Again he cautioned me about conversations with any LAPD reps without his presence.

Ruth told me Manny needed me in the conference room. I went in, and Manny was standing by our rolling three-by-five whiteboard, marker in one hand and clipboard in the other. A stack of printouts was scattered on the table. He was making an organizational chart with colored marker lines connecting boxes with names in them. On closer look, I recognized Candace and Cooper. An asterisk appeared on names in five of the six boxes. He underlined four boxes and put a question mark next to nine other names.

"Good, you're here," he said.

"What's this?"

Manny explained his chart and how Cooper's different Facebook accounts consisted of the same four or five persons using fake names and personas to lure suckers in. I waved him off when he started to tell me how it worked. "Did you come up with a group running the show?" I asked.

"Three for sure, besides Cooper, maybe a fourth. One is probably a female who does a lot of trolling, phishing for credit cards and SS numbers."

"What makes you think it's a woman?"

"Shopping sites visited, things purchased," he explained. *And I thought I was smart.*

"Or a drag queen. Any real names, addresses, phones?"

"A half-dozen numbers, burner phones. Your buddy Pete Gunn might be able to tell you where the phones were bought, maybe used a credit card. But I got a friend who might do something for us." He grinned. "Maybe turn the tables on these dickwads."

"Legal?"

"Of course not. That's why the guy charges so much." Again, with the grin.

"What will five Benjamins get us?"

"He'll dump a bunch of malware on them so you can read all the stuff on their computers and phones for half that. But his is a 'cash only' operation."

"Do it!"

"Yowza, boss."

A little after eight o'clock that night, Linda and I were munching popcorn watching Bogie pursue *the things that dreams are made of* on PBS when my cell rang. I hit pause on the TV remote and picked up my cell. The caller ID said "Ed Russell."

"This is Rollo."

"She never came back from Santa Monica, her phone is still off, and her car still shows on Third Street." His voice was filled with panic.

"Where are you, home?"

"Yes."

"Go find her car, don't touch anything, call the police, then me. I'll be in the vicinity and meet you there." I then called detective Dan Tankersley and told him my client might be missing, and if so, I'd be in touch.

Linda heard my half of both conversations, making faces as I spoke. She followed me as I went to the bedroom to change out of my pajamas. "Where you going?" she asked as I pulled on jeans.

"Santa Monica's Third Street Mall. Last known location of one of my clients," I said, stepping into my boots.

"What kind of case are you working on?"

"Blackmail," I said, wrestling my black hoodie over my arms and head.

"I thought Dan Tankersley was a homicide detective?"

"Yep. But it seems my only suspect got himself murdered last week, and one of my blackmail victims is possibly missing." Slipping my .380 auto into my back pocket, I kissed her goodbye and headed out the door.

Her "Keep me posted" wasn't a request.

# CHAPTER 16

## LOVE LOST

**ED RUSSELL WAS** engaged in a heated exchange with two Santa Monica patrol officers when I arrived at the Third Street Mall. Their raised voices and flashing blue and red lights bouncing off car windows drew a small crowd in the mall's parking structure. Ed spotted me and shouted, "Michaels, get over here!"

When I rushed over, one of the officers fronted me with a *sick of this crap* attitude on his face. "Shut up, Ed, and calm down," I said, trying to step around the officer to get to my client, who was now threatening lawsuits. "Look, Officer, let me calm my client down." He did. Ed didn't.

"Can you believe these guys? They say there's not much they can do, for god's sakes!"

I put my hands on his shoulders and whispered, "Lower your voice, Ed. The only thing you are doing is slowing things down. Did you tell them the reason we think she was here?"

"No way," he whispered back.

"The police won't do much without a compelling circumstance. We have to tell them what we think is going on. Her life might depend on it."

"We don't know anything," he said, no longer whispering. "All we know is that Candace received a text from this area at nine this morning and drove here this afternoon. Once here, she phoned the same text sender then turned her phone off. That was over eight hours ago!" The pitch of his voice reached new heights.

"If you won't tell the officers, I will," I threatened.

"And I'll fire your ass!" Ed shouted, causing the two officers to spin around and head over.

"In that case, Ed, I quit," and turned to the approaching officers. Ed listened while I explained what I knew to the officers. I didn't mention the ex-boyfriend was a murder victim and blackmailer. The earful I gave them included Detective Tankersley's cell number for credence. I wondered if I'd still be able to call Tank a friend after tonight. I'd also have to check with my lawyer/partner, Art, to see if I just violated our confidentiality agreement with Ed and Candace Russell.

The officers contacted a supervisor who brought their on-duty detective to the scene. And one of them called Tankersley. This chain of events lasted an hour, during which I reached Peter Gunn to get precise times for the calls to and from Candace Russell's cellphone.

The on-scene detective approved my earlier suggestion to the lieutenant to check security camera recordings within the time parameters of Candace's arrival at the parking structure. The security cameras captured Candace's entrance, third-floor parking, and meeting up with an unknown woman, who seemed vaguely familiar to me. They walked to the elevator, getting off on the ground floor, to go we know not where. *Do I know the woman Candace met, maybe saw her before?* A second look at the recording didn't help. That Candace met with a woman explained why she would agree to a meeting.

Ed and I accompanied an officer and made a walk-through search of the mall floors to no avail. We then wound up at Santa Monica Police HQ for some tough questioning interspersed with repeated calls to his wife's phone. Periodic checks on her car proved fruitless until 11:20. The car was gone! Ed's phone showed her car now parked at home, but her cell was still off. We had wasted three hours of Santa Monica PD's time. After a heated dressing-down, they bid us both a bon adieu!

I was happy, but Ed was pissed. Indeed at his wife, but mostly at me. As we walked to the police parking lot, he unloaded. "I told you not to say anything to the police. Now you have me and my wife caught up in a murder case, endangering my reputation and discrediting my firm. Millions are involved. You're an incompetent ass. You're fired!" His face twisted in anger, and I thought or hoped, he would throw a punch.

I got right in his face and watched his eyes get big when I put my hand on his chest and gave him a little shove, forcing him to take two steps back to keep from falling on his ass. "This isn't *The Apprentice*, Ed, and you sure as hell aren't Donald Trump. I've already quit, remember?"

He raised his hands, palms out, in supplication. "Sorry," he said, "just blowing off steam."

"Listen, and listen good, the only thing the police know is your wife had an affair with this asshole, and he got offed a year after you and your wife patched things up. But Tankersley, he's a different story. He'll come knocking with questions to which he already has answers. If you and Candace don't come clean, who knows? Leaks happen."

"You know him by reputation?"

"We're longtime buds. We worked on a couple of joint task force operations together. Think 'dog with a bone'—gets his teeth in it and won't let go."

"Will you go with Candace and me to see this guy tomorrow?"

"You forgetting I quit already?" I said with a smile. "Let's go talk with your wife."

O   O   O

I followed Ed out the Pacific Coast Highway to his and Candace's gated community a little after Malibu. We stopped at the guard enclosure, and Ed told the gate-keeper to let me follow him without the usual rigmarole. We made a quick right on a narrow lane where large two-story homes, packed close together on cliffs, enjoyed a five-million-dollar view of the Pacific. About two hundred yards down, we made a left. A parking lot ran the width of the house, probably eighty or ninety feet. A car sat in front of the entry with the trunk lid up. Ed parked his electric Lexus on one side and I parked my gas guzzler on the other. Two suitcases filled the open trunk of what I assumed was Candace's Tesla. If so, I didn't think she was going on vacation.

We entered the home, and I turned from PI to referee in less than a minute. Pent-up acrimony rushed to the surface. They shouted hurtful accusations back and forth. Ed swept the tchotchkes from the mantle to the floor, causing me to signal for a timeout. Ignored. I forcefully shouted, "STOP!"

They both spun in my direction, wide-eyed and flushed with anger. "Come on, people, this gets us nowhere. Please, let's cool down and act like adults. Ed, go to the kitchen and get some cold libations." I pointed to Candace and barked, "You! Sit down on that couch," and she snapped to it. "Now tell me what happened when you got the text from the bad guys and why you didn't notify Ed or me."

"Later," she whispered as Ed returned from the kitchen carrying three sweating bottles of Yuengling beer, sans tops. We each took a slug. Maybe Candace only sipped.

I wiped the beer foam from my 'stache and told Ed, "Your wife was just going to tell us what the hell is going on and where she's been the past twelve hours."

"My husband seems to know wherever my car is, who I call, or who calls me. I had no idea he was spying on me. Our marriage has no trust. I didn't stray until I overheard an intern telling another coworker she had a thing going on with Ed. The girl she talked to said she spent a weekend in Vegas with him over a year ago. I'm done with this." When she got up and headed to the door, Ed grabbed her by the arm.

"You're not leaving 'til you tell us about the text you got this morning," he said, which signaled round two, and they were back at it again. Candace broke free and threw her beer at him, bottle and all.

As she slammed the door on the way out to her car, I stopped Ed from chasing after her and told him to let her go; I'd follow her. She burned fifty feet of rubber and a bunch of electricity with her Tesla and sped down the lane. I wondered if I was being paid enough for this as I got into my ride.

# CHAPTER 17

## TOO CLOSE

**THE PACIFIC COAST** Highway wasn't entirely deserted a little after one thirty in the morning as I followed Candace Russell's Tesla back toward the way Ed and I came over an hour ago. Tailing is an art form a seasoned dope cop taught me during my stint in a Bureau Narcotics Unit. He explained that there are two types of targets, the clueless and the wary. You adjusted accordingly. You get too close, and you get made; too far back, you lose track.

Candace's left turn onto Topanga Canyon was a surprise and left me without the cover even sparse traffic provided. Topanga's many twists and turns meant I'd have to tighten up my tailing distance. About a mile into the canyon, we slowed down. A pickup truck appeared in my rearview mirror. *Where'd you come from*? Now we were three, and I was the middle car in a twenty-mph train. A few curves later, the clown behind me was now on my ass, double-tapping his brights as if wanting to pass.

The Tesla pulled to the side of the road. *Caution— or had she made me?* I hit my bright lights to mess with her night vision and giddy-upped around her Tesla. The pickup didn't follow. A zig and a zag had me around two curves, putting a quarter-mile between us. I made a hard left into a driveway and killed the lights. Thirty seconds later, Candace slowly drove by in her Tesla, closely followed by the now patient pickup truck, a beat-up crew cab. I backed out, hit the lights, and quickly caught up. Darkened windows hid who was in the truck's cab. Its plates were unreadable, splattered with mud, and a hard-cover concealed the inside of the bed.

Our three-vehicle caravan picked up speed where we could and slowed when cautious Candace deemed it necessary. We slowed cresting the final hill and started to descend into the San Fernando Valley. Suddenly, Candace pulled to the side of the road as if to let the following vehicles pass. But the pickup pulled directly behind her. I stopped in the roadway and hit my brights. The truck driver stuck out his arm to wave me around both vehicles. As I slowly drove past, the cab light came on while its passenger got out. They both looked rough around the edges, nothing like anybody Candy Russell would want to be seen with in polite company. The old sixth-sense had me pull over directly in front of her car, getting out as the big guy approached Candy's door, a revolver in hand. *Uh-oh!*

Somehow, my .380 peashooter was in my hand. The other muscle-shirted dipshit jumped from the truck behind a bright muzzle flash from a sawed-off shotgun in his hand. His shotgun's discharge put a severe hurt on his partner. He was trying to jack another round when two from my PPK took the shooter out, center mass. The pistol packer was writhing on the ground next to the Tesla, blood seeping through his pellet-tattered jeans, while he cried like a little bitch. I kicked his revolver under Candace's car so I wouldn't need to put one in his head. I wouldn't have minded doing it, but I had questions.

"Call an ambulance," he croaked.

I backhanded him with my gun hand to stop his whining, then put the still hot muzzle on his forehead. "First, you tell me what's going on with the lady in the car."

"Bitch stole something from us."

"Yeah, what?"

"My buddy's cellphone." My gun hand started to shake, making the gun barrel tap dance on the guy's forehead. "P-p-please don't shoot."

Adrenaline overload caused by this thirty-second life and death encounter was way too close a call and would probably shorten my time on earth by a few years. I put the Walther back in my pocket. It was then I heard the muffled screams of my client. I tried the door to her car. She still had it locked, and she still screamed. I tapped on the window and shouted, "It's over, Candace. It's all over!" I took out my phone and let the screen light up my face, and the window came down.

The screams gave way to sobbing and a bunch of weeping "Thank yous" directed to God's ear. I punched in 911.

"What is your emergency?" But all I could think was how pissed Linda was going to be. "Hello, hello? This is the 911 operator. What is your emergency?"

What I told the operator didn't have the effect on her that it had on me. She coolly got the info out of me that I was having trouble giving, but she hadn't just killed somebody. And she'd be home, sleeping long before I would be.

# CHAPTER 18

## A NEW PLAYER

**_I SPENT MOST_** of Monday morning explaining my Friday night and most of Saturday to Clancy at Art's request. Clancy would be joining the Russell case because of the weekend's complications. A half-dozen phone calls from inquiring minds, mostly Dan Tankersley, interrupted the telling. During his third call, I figured he needed something to do, so I asked, "Did you run ballistics on the revolver?"

His "What revolver?" made my head spin. *WTF Tank?*

"The one the other asshole was holding when I shot the guy with the sawed-off." I figured that should keep Tank busy for the rest of the day.

By early afternoon, the LAPD detectives, in conjunction with the Santa Monica PD and Sheriff's Homicide, concluded I had interrupted an attempted kidnapping of Candace Russell during the early morning hours of Saturday. Or so Art said, trying to cheer me up as we ate lunch in the conference room at Michaels & Associates. "You're not going to eat those fries?" he asked.

"I got enough grease from the Reuben. Swap you the fries for your pickles." And the deal was done. "When's the coroner's inquest? I'd like to get my gun back," I said, wiping grease from my hands on one of the paper towels from the stack that came with our meal.

"You're talking weeks, if not months. You have six more handguns in the safe," he said, squeezing the last ketchup packet onto the fries. "Linda taking you for tomorrow's hospital thing?"

"Yes. We'll probably be there most of the day, and I hope to be back here by Thursday."

Ruth entered and handed me a business card imprinted with "Lita A. Combs, Licensed Private Investigator." It included a PO Box and a 213 phone number. "She said she's here at the request of Candace Russell." The lack of a business address had me guessing she worked out of her car like a character from a Michael Connelly crime novel.

"Show her to my office while I clean up."

Being an ace detective, I immediately recognized Combs as the woman who met Candace at the mall Friday afternoon. Smiling, she stood, thrust out her hand, and said, "Sergeant Michaels, remember me?" clearing up why she looked familiar to me on the mall videos: she had to be an ex-copper from my past. Her grip and stature told me she had a gym membership and used it.

"No, Ms. Combs," I lied. "Have we met?"

"A couple of times when we both wore the badge. But that's not why I'm here. Mrs. Russell told me all about her Saturday morning adventure and you saving her ass from God knows what," she said, returning to her seat. Her glasses had an expensive light rose tint, and her hair was swept back behind her ears.

"So, where do you fit in with all of this?" I asked, taking my seat.

"Her divorce attorney has retained me to clarify a couple of legal issues regarding representation and to determine if you'll agree to share information."

That surprised me. "Perhaps I should bring in the attorney the Russells retained to represent them in another matter," I said and picked up the phone to ask Ruth to have Art join us.

When I put the phone down, Combs asked, "Were you following Mrs. Russell at her husband's request?"

I smiled. "Let's not get ahead of ourselves, Lita." Of course, Art would turn her down, but the fencing might uncover something we could use. It didn't, and Art amicably agreed to talk to Candace's new attorney. It didn't last long, Lita quickly realizing we wouldn't be forthcoming with details. She left us to go to Kaufman & Russell to serve Ed's divorce papers. I thought about calling him with a heads-up but opted for tails, sure that Lita was being well paid to get it done.

I filled Art in on my suspicion that private eye Combs wasn't only involved in Candy's divorce case and was probably hired by Candy to identify the blackmailers and recover Cooper's phone.

"You think they got the phone?" Art asked.

"Why else meet in Santa Monica?" And Art left to call the new lawyer.

I made a few calls of my own to ask around about Combs. I was told she retired from LAPD after graduating from law school and passed the bar on her second try. One source told me she was a "hired-gun type" not afraid of getting her hands dirty. Manny told me she kept a low profile on social media, presenting herself as a professional licensed and bonded private investigator on her LinkedIn page. I taped her card into my Rolodex.

Two hours later, Ed Russell was in my face waving divorce papers and a subpoena for a restraining order hearing set for Friday. The world immediately around him had been spinning out of his control since Friday. The divorce filing was dated the previous Monday, meaning his wife played him all along since the Russells brought Art and me on board. What if she was doing it from the get-go?

"Where's my wife?" he demanded.

"We don't know, Ed. You want us to find her?"

"What the hell am I paying you guys for? I need to see her before she gets that restraining order. Find her!" He stormed out of my office, heading toward the elevator. I gave chase.

"What about the videos?"

"That's the least of my worries. Some of my case files are missing from our house. Find her, and you'll find the files. She probably has Cooper's phone, too. She withdrew five thousand from one of our accounts Friday." We both got on the empty elevator, and he pressed P for parking.

I reached around him and pressed L. "We need to talk, Ed. Let me buy us a cup of coffee." He exhaled and nodded.

Ernesto was preparing to close shop, and we had the place to ourselves. I bombed an Americano with a double-shot espresso while Ed went with a cappuccino. I put a twenty on the counter and told Ernesto to keep the change. He flipped the "Closed" signs on both doors and disappeared to the small kitchen, seemingly to rattle pots and pans.

"Okay, Ed, this is where you tell me what the hell is going on."

"Our firm has a case that will rival Paraquat in scale, and a government cover-up is also involved. We also have insider information, possession of which could get us prosecuted. Our internal investigators are looking for leaks or signs of spying or intrusion into our data storage and communications. Saturday, I discovered two files were missing from my home office. Both contained information critical to our case. Now I think my wife's betrayal goes far beyond a dalliance with a porn freak."

"Why?"

His explanation was mostly conjecture, citing the timing of events, the final straw being the files missing from his home despite a top-of-the-line home security system. I detected pain and bitterness in his telling, and it seemed he was hurting more from misplaced love than ego bruising.

I knocked back my heavy dose of caffeine and said, "I'll do my best to find her, Ed, but I can't make her talk to you."

"I know," he said as we left, his coffee untouched.

I called Dan Tankersley. He told me LAPD Crime Lab hadn't checked the gun yet but would send the sheriff's lab a copy when available. He added that his boss wanted more because the Russell love story didn't do squat to solve the Cooper murder, broadening the scope instead of narrowing the focus.

My "Sorry, Tank" didn't get me an absolution.

I was getting that this case was turning into a divorce case complicated by blackmail and three dead bodies. At least the lying clients were no surprise. Most do.

# CHAPTER 19

## FAMILY MATTERS

***I DIDN'T KNOW*** what to expect from Linda when I entered the house a little before 7:00. The flowers on the table were starting to wilt, matching Linda's acceptance of the sincerity surrounding the giving. El Gato seemed glad to see me, or maybe it was the cooking smells of his favorite meal, fried chicken.

"Honey, I'm home!" wasn't met with enthusiasm.

"Kitchen" was what I got. I went in, and Baby Marlowe wiggled in her high chair harness, seemingly glad to see her dad. Linda sat at the table, a wineglass before her, a half-bottle of Chablis within reach. "You didn't call, so I started without you. Your plate's in the oven, salad's in the fridge. Help yourself."

"And how was your day?" I asked, grabbing the salad and a bottle of French dressing.

"Same-old-same-old. Laundry day, a little shopping. More importantly, how was yours?"

I removed the KFC box from the oven and ran my day down to her between bites and finger licks. She had no Qs or comments then, pouring herself more wine and fetching me another Coors, she said, "I've asked Mom to fly out and give us a hand."

"Good idea. When?"

"Wednesday, day after the surgery." Linda's mom was here for the birth of our daughter and proved a big help during Linda and Marlowe's first week at home.

"You fill her in on all that's going on?"

"I had to tell somebody, Rollo." And the tears flowed, crushing my soul.

I went to her, knelt beside her chair, and took hold of her hand. "I swear to you, Linda. This is my last case." Then my phone's ringtone told me Clancy was calling. Linda just shook her head. I took my salad and phone to the living room.

Putting Clancy on Lita Combs's trail led us to the elusive Mrs. Russell's hideout. He notified her husband first, then me, crowing about his tracking skills. In this business, things can change in a heartbeat. "Hang on, Rollo. Lita is coming out of the house with Mrs. Russell and a John Doe carrying two suitcases. Lita popped her trunk, John's stowing the luggage. He's joining Candy in the back seat. And we're going mobile. I'm betting Lita's taking them to an airport. Anyway, they won't be here when Ed Russell shows up—call him so he doesn't waste his time. I'll keep you posted."

Ed Russell let my call go to voice mail. "Pick up, Ed. Your wife just left the location with the woman who served you the divorce papers this afternoon. We're on it and will keep you posted."

Less than a minute later, he was screaming in my ear, demanding we do illegal acts to detain his wife. He was working himself up to an irrational state, firing a slew of expletives at me. I ended his call. I let him play with his redial button six times until he stopped calling.

I ate some salad for five minutes before I dialed him up. We connected, but he said nothing. Only his breathing said he was on the line. "Okay, Ed, let's get serious here. You know we can't do any of the things you suggested. Stay by the phone, and we'll update you every half hour."

"You guys are a big disappointment—I should've put my people on it. Your holier than thou bullshit… What if she's skipping town with my files?"

"What's in the files that's so scary?"

"Stuff she can use to fight our prenup agreement," he said, but I doubted it. Speculating on what was really in the files would be a waste of time, none of which would be billable. I ended the call by telling him to stand by for updates.

When I returned to the kitchen, mother and daughter were nowhere in sight, my chicken was cold, and the chill was gone from my beer. I didn't taste or savor what I ate or drank while contemplating the state of my marriage and my desire to make Linda and Marlowe happy by a career change. How the hell would a guy like me handle a nine-to-five gig of any kind? Clancy's ringtone snapped me out of the funk that was setting in.

"Speak," I said.

"Just as I thought, airport. Burbank, to be precise. Lita dropped them off at the curb and split. I went into the terminal. Mrs. Russell and John Doe depart for Vegas in twenty minutes. I snapped some good pics. Maybe Russell knows the guy his wife is skipping town with. Want I should go?"

"Yes. Don't forget receipts for everything. I think Ed Russell will want to join you. I'll fill him in. No gambling and no escorts."

"The only reason I joined this outfit was for all the fun you said we'd have. Did you lie to me? Now I'm catching a plane to Sin City, and you're telling me I can't sin? Geez!"

I called Ed Russell with the news, instantly turning him into a class-A jerk. "I'm not paying you guys to go to Vegas. That's on you. You could have stopped her out in the Valley."

"My guy's already on the plane, Ed, two rows back of Candace."

"You should have done what I asked."

"Remember the retainer you signed with us? You said 'follow her,' so that's what we're doing. The retainer has a clause that informs the client that all the communications between us are subject to recording. There's more, Ed, so stop being a dick, and let me finish—she's with a guy."

"What guy?"

"Not ID'd yet, but I'll send you his picture. Let me know if you recognize him. I'll call with their location once our operative has it. I assume you'll go there to confront her about the files. My man will be a great witness if that's what you want."

"Send me the picture." I did, but he never called back to acknowledge receipt or recognition.

An hour later, Clancy called again, saying Candace and her John registered at the Rio as Mr. and Mrs. Robert Anderson of Santa Monica. He also left that info on Ed's voice mail.

After listening to Clancy and wishing him a "Sleep tight," I tried Ed's number, but his phone was not in service.

Tomorrow I was scheduled to have my bone marrow infused into my daughter, hoping to save her life. I turned my phone off and headed for the bathroom to get my mind and body right. A twenty-minute steaming hot shower washed the day's grime and tensions away, but not the racing thoughts in my head. I wiped the steam from the mirror, thinking I would shave. The guy looking back said, "Fuggedaboutit!"

I put on clean underwear and padded into the kitchen to fetch cookies and milk. El Gato then followed me to the couch to lap milk from my glass while I watched TV news. After confirming the Dodgers were still the hottest team in sports, we went to bed.

Checking the clock every five or ten minutes had me doze off around 2:00. I was jolted awake by the alarm at 5:00. The snooze button got me Linda's elbow at 5:15. We were out the door at 5:55, Linda behind the wheel, Marlowe sleeping strapped in her car seat. Yours truly slumped half-awake in the front passenger seat.

# CHAPTER 20

## DONOR

**HOSPITALS WERE NEVER** my thing. I was born in one, as were my three children. My many unhappy and painful visits far outnumbered those happy events. Injuries and illnesses of friends and loved ones were the worst. But often, duty called me to interview a victim of a heinous crime to get a statement or a dying declaration or pull back a sheet for a parent to identify a dead child. Memories of my near-death experiences requiring weeks of hospital time now conjure up visions of wives, children, and friends putting on forced smiles of encouragement.

I'd be lying if I said I wasn't nervous about today's visit. The what-ifs kept me awake most of the night, and I hadn't taken a Valium or aspirin for three days, and my caffeine jones raged as we pulled up to the entrance to Cedars. Marlowe still slept as I leaned across the seat and kissed Linda. I got out and said, "See you later, sweetheart." Two cars had pulled in behind us to discharge passengers. Was this the ubiquitous 7:00 a.m. check-in time? Did I need to go through that stupid check-in procedure again? My angst was building, and my hand shook reaching for the door. *Get it together, Michaels!*

An hour later, I lay naked on a gurney while a young lady shaved part of my right leg and hip, and a corner of a sheet covered my privates. I thought she had copped a peek and felt compelled to tell her it was freezing in here. Smiling, she applied an iodine solution as an aftershave. After my hairless orange ass and hip were dry, they covered me with the rest of the sheet and a pre-warmed blanket, then rolled me to a staging area. The anesthesiologist told me about the happy juice he had in store for me, and a nurse hooked me up with an IV. The doctor I met last week came by and told me the company line again. "Any questions, Mr. Michaels?"

I stifled a yawn and said, "Can a guy get a cup of coffee in this place?" A promise of coffee and a light breakfast was given. Doc Happy Juice returned with a syringe of "Don't Give-a-Damn." Five minutes later, they slid me onto a stainless steel table under bright lights. A soft-speaking nurse stuck a thingy in my nose attached to an oxygen tube. People I couldn't see said nice things to me as they unwrapped me. Ego again had me trying to tell them the table was icy cold, but my mouth no longer did my bidding. "Sleep well, Mr. Michaels," were the last words I heard.

I awoke to the aroma of fresh-brewed coffee and a gentle hand on my shoulder. "Mr. Michaels, I'm going to raise you up so you can drink your coffee."

I opened my eyes to subdued lighting, taking a few seconds to focus and let reality set in. The nurse looked younger than the girl Brandon took to his high school prom this year. A bad case of cotton mouth kept me from saying yes, so I nodded. I worked my mouth for some moisture and lip-synced a plea for water. She smiled, holding a straw to my lips, and I hungrily drank.

"Easy, sir. Save room for your coffee."

"How did it go?" I asked as she put the glass down and handed me the magic elixir.

"Be careful, sir. It's hot," she said, avoiding an answer. My left forefinger was hooked to a monitor, and a pressure cuff had my bicep, but the oxygen hose was gone from my nose. "You're in the recovery room, and the doctor will be here soon to answer your questions. Says here you have breakfast coming, probably scrambled eggs and wheat toast."

The coffee was excellent. "And more coffee." Her smile seemed more genuine this time, leaving as the doctor entered. She wore the same uniform of green scrubs, dangling a stethoscope from her neck, and a surgical mask under her chin. "How did it go, Doctor?"

"We got what we came for, and the donor survived." Her smile matched the glint in her eyes. "And how are you feeling, Roland?"

"Thought I'd hurt more."

"We extracted enough marrow from your hip, leaving your femur for another time. The lab found nothing wrong with your healthy marrow, so very rich in stem cells. It's going to give your daughter a chance at a healthy life. Cases of aplastic anemia related to pregnancy and childbirth respond well to this therapy. By the time your daughter's case was discovered, harvesting stem cells from blood donors rarely works. Your matching marrow gives her the best chance for complete recovery. Let's hope this is the last time we do this."

"Amen, Doc."

Breakfast arrived in the form of an egg sandwich, coffee, and OJ, delivered by a gushing Diana. "Doctor says everything went great. Thank you, thank you, thank you, Rollo," she said, placing the tray on my lap and throwing her arms around me in a hug. Naturally, her exuberance spilled the coffee, the tray catching most of it.

"Careful, girl," I said, feeling a warm splash soak through to my iodine-coated ass. She didn't let go. Now, I felt her tears and sobs. I held her close and fought tears of my own.

o  o  o

That night, over inch-thick ribeyes, Linda brought up the four-hundred-pound gorilla in the room. "When are you going to tell Marie and, especially the kids, about their extended family members?"

My stomach reacted before my mouth did. Sometimes reality sucks. "Don't know if I want to talk about it tonight. You think the time is right?"

"I think everyone has the right to know. I'd be pissed if you hadn't told me, and I found out from someone else."

"You're right. I get it. How about I break the news to them this weekend?"

"How about tomorrow?" She gave me *the look,* and I nodded.

# CHAPTER 21

## FESSING UP

**MOST FATHERS WORRY** about what their kids think of them. Before Wednesday's encounter with Melissa and Brandon, my angst had me in knots. The hangover from Tuesday's trip to Cedars Surgery Center was probably a contributing factor. I don't think I could've done it without Linda's support. All my fears vanished with the kids' positive reactions.

I started from the beginning, with Linda's presence to keep me honest. First, the army and my time in Georgia. Of dating a young lady for a couple of months before leaving to seek fame and fortune in California. As I told my kids, I imagined the Temptations singing me their classic *"Papa Was a Rollin' Stone."* Their facial expressions registered surprise more than shock, understanding without rancor and recrimination. They, too, wondered why Diana never sought me out and why she wasn't bitter. I told them I didn't think Di was wired that way. More questions followed. Who does Leigh look like? And Laura? How old? Where do they all live? They asked their questions with excitement. I was grateful Linda helped with the answering and ventured positive impressions of her meeting the three new family members.

I then explained the "why now: part of Di seeking me out 23 years later and Laura's situation. Yesterday's bone marrow transplant in Cedars hospital, the sterile room, the waving through the observation window, and the weeks of hospitalization Laura was facing.

They were anxious to meet their adult sibling. And even more insistent on meeting their niece. Tomorrow was up to Di and Laura, so I made the call. Two o'clock was the decision.

"What about Mom?" Mel asked, taking my breath away.

My mouth opened, sucking in some air to answer, but Linda spoke up. "Your dad is going over to tell her now while the three of us wait here. When he gets back, I'll order us some Chinese takeout." They all looked at me, expecting I don't know what. I got up from the couch and headed to the door, my marrow-depleted hip registering pain for the first time. Was something puckering? The sour taste in my mouth came with the thoughts of what lay ahead.

"Good luck, Dad," my insightful daughter said.

I can't say it went well with Marie as I rushed through the story of Georgia, Diana, and the discovery of a daughter in need. She showed no surprise, disappointment, or anger. But what she had to say blew me away.

"I knew all along. We were struggling to make things work when you got out of the army, the miscarriage and all. But the future looked bright, you joining the police department, the new house, and all I dreamed about was in reach. Then the letter…" She choked back tears.

"What letter?"

"The letter from her," she exclaimed, her tears now flowing, "saying she was pregnant."

"Where's the letter?

"I burned it. Don't you see, it would ruin everything we were working for?" she moaned, her face twisted in pain.

I took her hand, knowing full well the pain she felt was my doing. "I'm sorry, Marie. It's not your fault that any of this happened. It's mine."

O　O　O

So here we are at the hospital, seven visitors masked up like stagecoach robbers. We stand on one side of a large window, waving hellos. Laura is on the other side, beaming a brave smile at us. Happy introductions are made of a brother and two sisters Laura never knew existed two weeks ago. These joyous moments flew by too quickly, and soon it was time to leave.

In the parking lot, we pledged to make more visits happen and said our goodbyes to go separate ways. Before we drove away, a calm enveloped me. I squeezed Linda's hand and whispered, "I love you," in her ear, and Marlowe giggled from the back seat.

Linda turned to me and asked, "Where the hell was the Laura's husband?"

The moment passed. I let go of her hand and answered, "I didn't ask, but I could see something was on Diana's mind. Just what, I couldn't tell."

"I think she was overwhelmed by it all. She seemed to take a special shine to Marlowe. Maybe thought of what might have been if Laura had grown up with a father."

"But Laura did. Di told me Mr. Wright is a wonderful father to Laura."

# CHAPTER 22

## HEART ATTACK

**CLANCY RETURNED TO** La-La Land yesterday since Ed Russell failed to meet him at the Rio Hotel and refused to return our calls. But he wasn't empty-handed. The resourceful Clancy managed to get photos of Candace and her roommate and a screenshot of the guest registry, identifying our J. Doe as Robert Anderson of Santa Monica. It's incredible how some smooth talking and a hundred-dollar bill gets an underpaid desk clerk's assistance.

Thursday morning, a lawyer from the Russell & Kaufman law firm called Art and requested a final report with a billing statement. Art told him he had to hear it from the horse's mouth. We decided I would storm their law offices and brace Ed Russell to find out what was going on.

As I entered, the young lady behind the front desk gave me a smile of recognition and greeting. "Hello again, Mr. Michaels."

I flashed the dimple and the folder and said, "I have some paperwork for Ed's secretary."

"I'll take it to Ms. Shaw if you don't mind. They were displeased the last time you got past me."

"These papers are my job app and résumé. Just tell Ms. Shaw I'm heading her way," I said over my shoulder.

I hustled down the long hallway. As I passed her desk and reached for the door, Ed Russell's secretary said, "Stop, Rollo. You can't barge in there."

"Sure I can."

I could tell right away that Ed wasn't used to people entering without being announced. My shock and awe tactic had the desired effect. Ed's face showed his surprise and discomfort as he struggled for words to form a sentence. "Wha-what…are you…" I dropped the photos of his wife and Robert Anderson enjoying each other's company in the lounge at the Rio Hotel. His red-faced embarrassment quickly turned into a tight-lipped grimace, and his hands shook with anger as he ripped the eight-by-ten photo copies in half.

"I take it you know this guy, right?" Two of his people rushed through the door, interrupting Ed's affirmative nod. He waved them off before it got physical and gestured for me to have a seat. They left, and I said, "Why aren't you returning our calls?"

"It's complicated. Although my name is on the door, Kaufman removed me from the big case as lead attorney and told me to settle my divorce case. Our investigators convinced him my wife has taken some of our files on the case and leaked them to the other side."

"And who's the guy sharing a suite at the Rio with your wife?"

"When you sent me the photos, I lost it and sent one of our investigators to Vegas to check it out." Pointing to the ripped photos on his desk, he continued, "This Anderson prick joined us right out of law school. We fired him about two years ago for sharing a client's confidential info to a gossip reporter. Last I heard, he was chasing ambulances on the West Side."

"The West Side, like in Santa Monica?"

"Yes, a small storefront operation, just off the boulevard. What difference does it make? He and his partner handle whatever walks in."

"Who is handling your wife's divorce petition?"

He pulled out the papers and flipped through them. "Holy shit!" he shouted as he grabbed at his chest and pulled at his tie. The door behind me flew open, and his Ms. Shaw rushed in as Ed slumped to the floor. She ran to his side, flung open a drawer in Ed's desk, and pulled out a pill bottle. "Call an ambulance!" she ordered.

I did the 911 on my cell and gave the particulars. Stroke or heart attack? I'd leave it up to the paramedics as Ed's secretary forced a nitro tab into his mouth and worked to bring him back around, removing his tie and opening his shirt. We made eye contact as she put her ear to his chest and listened to his heart. "It's beating too fast."

Two more people entered as Ed's eyes fluttered open, and he attempted to rise. They assisted him into his chair while Ed asked, "What happened, Michaels?"

"I'll let the ambulance folks tell you, Ed. They'll be here shortly."

"I don't need an ambulance." He attempted to stand, wobbled, and thought better of it. He gulped for air, working his jaw like a fish out of water. The people in the room sang a chorus of cautions to him as Shaw poured him a glass of water. The room went quiet when a diminutive man walked in. Neither his three-piece suit nor his face had a wrinkle. He had to be the other name on the door, Kaufman.

"You are going to the hospital this time, Ed. No ifs, ands, or buts." All heads bobbed in unison, even mine and Ed's. The ambulance crew soon arrived and whisked Ed away, and Kaufman ordered Shaw to follow and keep the firm posted on developments.

Samuel Ambrose Kaufman was right out of central casting. A full head of silver-white hair, blue eyes accentuated by a tan not out of a bottle, and a neatly trimmed white mustache. He turned to me, took an obligatory look at his Rolex, showing off at least an ounce of gold cufflink, and said, "You must be the private investigator who saved Ed's wife from kidnappers. I wonder if we may talk."

"Sure, as long as you're not going to charge me by the hour."

He smiled, closed the office door, and sat at Ed's desk. He pointed at the chair in front, and I played along, taking a seat.

"What did you say to Ed that made his heart react?" he asked as I steadied my breathing to calm my fight or flight adrenalin spike.

"It wasn't a love story, that's for sure," I said.

"So, you're working on his divorce case?"

"Michaels & Associates doesn't do divorce work. But I can't talk to you about any conversation with a client, as you are aware."

"So my partner of seventeen years lied to me?"

"Not being privy to what he told you, how can I say?"

"He said he had you following his wife. I assumed it had to do with their divorce."

"As I said, we don't do divorce."

"So, it must be about the missing files. Any progress?"

"Any answer would be a confirmation of your alternate assumption. So I can see you seek answers to questions I can't answer without violating Ed's trust. I can tell you it is a criminal matter not related to the theft of your files," I said, wondering if maybe they both could be.

He picked up the phone and punched in two numbers. "Heather, it's me. Tell Eric I'm waiting for him in Ed's office." He hung up and refocused on me. "Eric is ex-FBI and heads up our investigative team. I've assigned him to get to the bottom of the missing files. Ed insists his wife is behind the theft because of her divorce action and their prenuptial agreement. The involvement of Robert Anderson further complicates things. I was hoping you could work with our people on this."

"Not without Ed's and his wife's okay," I replied as the firm's head investigator tapped on the door and walked in, followed by one of the muscle guys from earlier. "They here to throw me out?"

"Of course not, Mr. Michaels, but your visits to our firm have been disruptive, to say the least. Your manner and actions could even be said to have caused my partner's heart attack. I thought Eric should get to know you if you decide to come on board and help us. Or bar your entry if you don't. Think it over, Mr. Michaels." Kaufman stood. "Eric, please show Mr. Michaels the way out."

Eric dismissed muscle-guy, and as we walked to the elevators, said, "Trying to serve two masters has me between a rock and a hard place here, Michaels, and I could use your help,"

"So, you're the one Ed sent to Vegas to check on his wife's tryst. You have a law degree?"

"Yeah, why?"

"A couple of reasons. First off, you know I can't tell you why Mr. and Mrs. Russell hired me. Secondly, I don't know you and you don't know me, in spite of what your IT people found on the internet. Or whatever my FBI file says."

"Okay, I get it," he said, pressing the down button.

"Did you know the guy Mrs. Russell shared a king-sized bed with at the Rio is also her divorce attorney? If I were you, I'd stick with Kaufman."

"Wow," he said, shaking his head watching as I got on the elevator and pressed the "P" button.

# CHAPTER 23

## TIDY KNOTS

**I FOLLOWED UP** on my client's trip to the emergency room at California Hospital on Grand where I found his secretary, Ms. Shaw, in tears. Ed was on life support in ICU, having suffered another attack during the ambulance ride from Spring Street. She said the crew thought they lost him five minutes out. "I just got off the phone with Mr. Kaufman's assistant, Heather. Nobody can get hold of Candace. The doctors wanted to know more about his medical history. The only thing I could tell them was his cardiologist's name."

"Maybe I can help," I said, taking out my phone. I called Linda and asked her to pull Alita Combs's number from my Rolodex. I called and told Alita what was happening at the hospital and the need to get the info to Ed's wife. And she was all over it.

"Thank you, Rollo. How did you get involved in all of this?" Ms. Shaw asked.

"A friend gave my number to your boss, and the Russells hired me. Do you have any idea of what's involved here?"

"Divorce?"

I shook my head. "No, murder."

She gasped.

o o o

Back at Michaels & Associates, I masked again before entering. Ruth warned me two LASO detectives, Tankersley and Gamblin, were waiting in my office, enjoying coffee and the last of my donuts. Linda exited the makeshift nursery with Marlowe cradled in her arms. She pointed to the bottle of hand sanitizer on the corner of Ruth's desk. The expression on her face had me dutifully pumping some and rubbing it in before approaching to slip my mask down and kiss my wife and daughter. That done, I went to see what Tank wanted.

They sat in the two visitor chairs, flakes of maple glazing dotted their ties. I went to the coffee setup and poured a mug full as Tank said, "Thanks for closing the Cooper case for us. The gun matched."

"We're going to file murder one on the clown with the buckshot ass," was Gamblin's contribution.

I slid my mask off to sip caffeine and sat at my desk. "You're welcome, guys. Always glad to cooperate with my brothers in law enforcement."

"Bullshit!" was Gamblin's response. Tankersley only grinned.

"Didn't Valley Homicide file felony murder and attempted kidnapping?"

"We'll just tag on, but first, we need to talk to your clients," Tank said.

The telling of how my day has gone up to this point had both of them making faces and shaking their heads. I gave them Alita Combs as a contact for the missing Candace Russell. Bad blood still existed between Gamblin and me, but Tank offered his hand, which I gladly shook. "Mask up, guys. I want to introduce you to my baby daughter, Marlowe," I said.

We stepped into the outer office where Linda led an enthusiastic Tank and an uncomfortable Gamblin to the hand sanitizer then into the conference room/nursery to meet our daughter. Tank, a father of four, said he hoped Marlowe would take after Linda in every way and never pick up any of her father's character defects. Gamblin voiced his agreement.

o　o　o

Dinner was interrupted twice that night. First, Alita Combs called to thank me for siccing the two LASO detectives on her with questions about her involvement in the Cooper case.

She explained, "When I responded by asking, 'Who the hell is Cooper,' things got a bit heavy. I told them about going with Candace to the Santa Monica mall last week to get her phone back. The asshole lifted his shirt to show us a beat-up old six-shooter tucked in his waistband. So, I showed him mine, which was then in my hand."

"Old beat-up six-shooter?" I asked.

"Yep, you know, a revolver like the old-timers carried when we came on the job, remember? But the grips were missing from this one."

"So, you shoot the guy, take the phone, and save the client a bundle."

"After Candace verified it was the right phone, she hands him a wad of cash, and everyone leaves happy—her with the phone, the *Gangsta* with a bunch of cash, and me with five hundred for a little over an hour of work," she reported.

"How much cash?" I prodded.

"I don't know. The five bills she peeled off for me didn't make much of a dent. It looked to be a one-inch stack of bills."

"Did you ID the seller?"

"No, but I got the plate number off the pickup truck he was driving. Gave it to your buddies," she said.

"Describe him."

"Male black, late twenties, five ten, skinny—maybe 150—shaved head, no facial hair. Gold chains hanging out of his shirt. Gold hoop about an inch diameter, hanging from his left ear," she said as I wrote it down.

"Any tats?"

"None I could see, but he sure acted like some kind of ghetto gangbanger."

"You tell all this to the Sherriff Dicks?"

"They didn't ask. Why are you?"

"Loose ends. Thanks for the call, Alita. You think she'll hold off on the divorce, hoping her old man croaks, so she gets a bigger piece of the pie?"

"I would," Alita said.

"Ain't love grand," was my parting shot.

Linda put my dinner in the microwave to reheat my thick, juicy pork chop, green beans, and fried rice. The timer went off about the same time my phone ringer played, "*I Shot the Sherriff*," indicating my dinner would wait some more while Tankersley ragged on me. Linda sighed and left the room.

"If you keep asking for my help, I'll need to start charging you," I said.

"We got a problem," Tank said.

"We, like you and me, or we, like you and the idiot you work with?"

"Both, wiseass. Your girlfriend, Alita Combs, gave us a plate number to the pickup truck you got in a shoot-out with eight hours later. I tried calling her back, no answer. I left a voice mail and fired off a text. Nada."

"I was on the phone with her a few minutes ago. She told me the conversation she had with you but didn't tell you the guy she and Candace met with had a revolver sounding a lot like your murder weapon. He was a black man, maybe thirty, just like your victim's age. The guys in my shooting were Hispanics, also about the same age. You seem to have a few loose ends to tie up before you close your homicide case. Did you guys jump at the easy way out?"

"No wonder my partner hates your guts," was Tank's goodbye.

Linda's mom entered the kitchen and asked, "Is it always like this?"

I smiled. "Nah. Some nights, it can get busy."

# CHAPTER 24

## FINISH LINE

**THE FOLLOWING MORNING,** Candace Russell called Michaels & Associates to inform us her husband, Ed Russell, didn't see the sunrise this day. He was pronounced dead at 3:18 a.m., never regaining consciousness. She thanked me for "saving" her life and then terminated our services.

"What about the videos?"

Her response of "No longer an issue" confirmed my suspicion that she and Alita had actually recovered Cooper's phone and the guys in the pickup truck were only trying to get the ill-gotten phone back.

"Who should we send our bill to?" I asked.

"Kaufman said he'd pay it," and she was gone. Leaving me to wonder who *really* killed Cooper. My subconscious shot back, *Who besides Tankersley really cares?*

I filled my partners in, and Art had Ruth compile a bill for $15,900 and some change, less the ten-K retainer. It was in the outgoing mail before Ed Russell's body was at the mortuary.

As I sat in my office staring out the window at the Miracle Mile section of Wilshire Boulevard, I wondered what was next. I sipped a cup of dark roast and bit off a large piece of a maple glazed to fuel my musing.

What will my partners say when I tell them I am done with casework? Could I run the security end of Michaels and Associates? No, not fair to Mr. Clean. Maybe have Linda screen the incoming cases, allowing me to take only those she deemed safe? That would be wrong on so many levels. Corporate security? Law enforcement?

*"Captain Malinka on line two,"* Ruth announced over the intercom, ending my angst-building thoughts.

"Yo, Corinne, what's up?"

"I'm surprised the infamous Rollo Michaels has time for a peon like me. All that press coverage must keep the phones busy with wannabe clients."

'Yes, mostly horny damsels in distress. Is that why you called?"

"No, Rollo. I just called to tell you your buddy, Joe Roberts, is putting in his retirement papers."

"I'm surprised. Put me down for a couple of tickets to his retirement party."

"Not funny, Rollo. After his altercation with you and your complaint about him stalking your family members, the bureau chief wanted him sent for psych evaluation this week. When I called him in and relayed the message, he went ballistic on me, and my adjutant had to restrain him.

Like you said, 'Off the rails,' like. We red-flagged him and took his gun and badge, making him crazy again. When he finally calmed down, two of our detectives drove him and his car home. They took him inside the house, which they say was a shambles, and sat with him for half an hour until they felt he had it under control.

But when they returned to the station, one of them told me she spotted booking photos of you, your ex-wife, and crime scene pics of her house in Winnetka. He also had one of your house in Reseda, all stuck to his fridge."

"The asshole qualifies as a 51-50. Why not a straitjacket and involuntary commitment?"

"But wait, there's more. The detective telling me this was the one who caught the Cooper case about the time Roberts was looking for the victim in your wife's case. She had originally thought Cooper was a suicide and asked Joe for his opinion. She said Joe exploded, called her a dumb bitch, and told her it was a 187, and Rollo Michaels did it."

"He's been ordered to stay away from you and your family, and after Detective Kate Andrews told me of Joe's photo gallery, I contacted the CO of Mission Division to provide extra patrol to your ex's house. Figured you'd kick his ass again if he came by your house."

"Trust me. I'll do more than that. Have you given Marie a heads-up?"

"I was thinking it might be better coming from you." She paused as my blood pressure rose, then said, "Listen, Rollo, Roberts has friends in high places who'd love your head on a platter for putting Joe in the hospital. Many think you skated on the battery charge, so stay away from Roberts."

"I'll do whatever's needed to protect my kids and their mother. Marie never got her gun back after her trial, so I'll give her another one when I go there from work. She knows how to use it if he shows up. Based on what you told me, she'd be justified in using it. Thanks for the call, Cap," I said, ending the call.

The muscles in my back and shoulders were knotting up the more I thought of Joe Roberts. The vindictive bastard was a real threat. Thankfully, he couldn't use his police powers to screw over me and my family anymore, but he certainly wouldn't stop trying to hurt me. And I wouldn't put it past him to use insanity as a defense. A plan started forming in my head, but I feared time wasn't on my side. The last thing I wanted to do was sit on my ass and wait for Joe Roberts to make a move. Defense was never my strong suit. Knowing where he was would be a strategic advantage. I washed down three aspirin with tepid coffee and made a phone call to Pete Gunn. He agreed to rent me some equipment, at a discount, of course.

# CHAPTER 25

## HIGH TECH

**THAT IT WOULD** rain this night of all nights in the City of Angels was a boost to my morale. It provided cover for the illegal act I was about to do. A few minutes before two in the morning, I parked my Escalade on a side street a half block from Joe Roberts's home and set the keys on top of the left rear tire. I was in stealth mode, nothing in my pockets to make noise; my black hoodie, pants, and Skechers. Practically invisible in the gloom. As I walked on the other side of the street away from the street lighting, I turned the corner, and the sounds of traffic on the Ventura Freeway grew louder as I approached Joe's 1940s house. My target, his 2020 Ford Expedition, sat in the driveway in stark contrast to his dilapidated home. I crouched down low and looked for signs of life on the street or in Joe's house. Nada. One place had its windows open as the light and sound of a TV spilled out, barely reaching me.

I crab-walked to the rear of his SUV and slid out of my backpack. I fished around inside the pack and retrieved my penlight. I held the business end in my left fist and pressed the ON button, shielding any glare that might draw an insomniac's wandering eye. My little finger allowed enough lite within the pack to prepare the equipment Pete Gunn provided.

Today's tech was only in comic books when I was a kid. Pete's instruction seemed simple enough, just crawl under the car, tape the gizmo to the axle, turn it on, and beat feet without getting shot. He emphasized the alarm system on a Ford was easily triggered.

I crawled under the left rear, duct tape in one hand, the tracker in the other, and the penlight in my mouth. I had no idea what all the stuff was I was looking at, or for that matter, a place to attach the tracking device. I struggled to fit it here and there, finally opting close to the differential. Road crud and three years of grease and oil fought with the tape adhesive requiring multiple winds of tape around the fattest part of the rear axle. I was getting cramped working in such tight quarters. Every ripping off the duct tape seemed loud enough to wake the dead. I was nearly done when a car's headlights came around the corner, and a Valley Cab stopped at the curb in front of Joe's house, no more than thirty feet from me. I squirmed further under Joe's Ford.

Two people got out of the cab. I recognized Joe's voice but not the woman's. He paid the driver, and the taxi took off. Giggles and laughter sounded like they'd been partying, maybe even a bit drunk, as they headed up the walkway to his front door.

"Show me the money, or I'm not going in your house," the woman said.

"What? Are you going to walk home? I paid the escort service, Rosie," Joe said.

"That was for going to the party with you, Joey."

"Okay, Rosie, how much?"

"Two hundred?"

"How about fifty and breakfast in the morning?"

"A hundred only 'cause I like policemen, and you can drive me home to Cerritos in your big car after breakfast."

"Deal, sweet cheeks," he said, and the porchlight came on. Motion detector? Security cameras? He unlocked the door, and they went in.

She gave a little squeal and laughed. "Oh, Joey, you're so fresh." The door closed, and a minute later, the porchlight went out.

Interior lights revealed that all the window shades were drawn long before I arrived. I butt-scooted and repositioned myself to complete what I'd started. Nervous sweat burned my eyes as I wrapped what seemed like yards of tape, securing the battery pack and tracker. I switched it on, slipped out from under the SUV, and fled the scene.

When it rains, it pours. After I turned right onto Ventura Boulevard, a patrol car lit me up. I pulled to the curb as the rain came down harder. The police spotlight hit my mirrors, preventing me from seeing what was happening behind me.

*"Turn your engine off and step from your car. Keep your hands where we can see them,"* their loudspeaker blared.

I did neither. Instead, I turned my radio up to max and dropped the gearshift into reverse to give them something to worry about. I then lowered my window an inch, attached my interior video feed to my phone, and waited. When they got out of their cruiser, they'd get to meet Mr. Asshole.

*"Turn your engine off, Michaels, and get out of your car!"* they persisted. By using my name, they let the cat out of the bag. It seems some people never get the word. As Big Vinnie would say, "Fuggedaboutit!"

This failure to comply got them both out in the rain. I recognized the big guy as one of the two who broke my ribs and booked me for breaking Roberts's arm. This time, his partner was a 5' 6" young lady smart enough to wear raingear while Mr. Macho Man stepped up to my window to flex his biceps. "Get the fuck out of your car, dipstick, before I drag you out through the window."

As I lowered the window farther down, he jumped back and drew his gun. "I'm not playing games with a clown like you," I said. "I should tell you you're on candid camera and setting a poor example for your trainee. Be best if you'd call for a sergeant before your alligator mouth overloads your canary ass."

He holstered his weapon, ordered his trainee back in the car, and then said, "We ain't done yet, Michaels. We'll see you around."

"What's the matter, afraid I'd tell your sergeant you're an idiot? I bet he already knows that. You know, Gleason, you wouldn't make a pimple on a real cop's ass,"

I goaded. Surprisingly, he didn't take the bait. When he opened the cruiser door, I heard his radio blare an *"All Units"* call and watched them speed away, fishtailing on the rain-slicked boulevard.

# CHAPTER 26

## ANNOUNCEMENT

**AFTER AN UNEVENTFUL** weekend, the Monday morning I'd spent forty-eight hours working myself up for, arrived. There were no Joe Roberts sightings where he shouldn't be. And Pete Gunn's tracker said Joe's SUV only moved from his residence twice Saturday—to the Whole Foods Market on Riverside in the morning, then the promised trip to Cerritos in the afternoon. And yesterday, he drove to the Denny's in Panorama City.

Linda opted to have her mother babysit Marlowe today while we dropped the bomb on our fellow partners. My trepidations multiplied as the minute hand got closer to straight up. At three minutes to D-Day, Linda entered my office, asking, "You ready?"

"No. I feel sick."

"Man up, Rollo. How do you want to do this?"

"TCB first, then I'll gently break it to them during the talk around. You know we never talked about your plans."

"I'm with the guy who brought me," she said with a smile. "Let's get it over with." And we went to the conference room. As usual, Ruth and Manny would cover the office, while the meeting would be anything but usual.

First off, everyone was present for the first time in a long time. Linda started with the weekly figures, proudly announcing weekly billing exceeded fifteen thousand, excluding the Russell case, for the first time, making the mundane stuff easily ignored. Next, Mr. Clean announced hiring an office clerk and a salesman he described as an "ex-cop without attitude." Art reported pending negotiations with a new insurance carrier. Clancy updated his wife's status. "Sylvia has finished her chemo and will return to work in two weeks!" drawing cheers and applause from all. Now it was my turn.

"You all know the outcome of the Russell case and my resorting to deadly force, so there's no need to go there. Near-death experiences are not new to me, and they go with what I do. Linda has pointed out that I have obligations to her, but mainly to our daughter, Marlowe. She also hit on the recent discovery of a grown-up daughter who introduced me to my first grandchild. I hope you see her point when you add in my two teenagers from my first marriage. The Russell case will be my last case." They all just sat there in stunned silence.

Finally, Linda broke the ice. "I won't risk Marlowe's future on some fifty-dollar-an-hour bullshit. We bill the same for accident cases, background checks, missing persons, and everything Manny can do without leaving the office cases. I don't want to be a widow and have my daughter grow up without a father."

"We all get it, Linda, but Rollo and Clancy are detectives, and clients pay for their expertise…it's what they do," Art said.

"Too much of what we do deals with criminals. Every time I enter his office, I see the bullet holes in his desk, reminding me of all the scars on his body," she shot back.

"It's the business we chose. Crime is out of control, and recent press has business booming," Art replied.

"We'll need to raise rates and what we're paying to keep up with demand. Corporate gigs are offering benefits to retired coppers," Mr. Clean added.

"No, Jack, I think I speak for everyone here when I say you're not getting a raise," I said, getting a few laughs from the gathering.

Keeping with the break in the tension, Clancy chimed in with, "Well, if you're stepping down, partner, maybe we could bring Joe Roberts in, now that he's retiring," causing Linda to gather up her folders and leave the room.

My "Now you see what I'm up against" signaled the end of the meeting. I'd laid out the issue for all to see, but my partners would deal with the particulars later. I returned to my office to find Linda sitting at my desk with a cup of coffee and a donut.

"I don't think the boys believe you," she said.

"We'll see. It was easier handling accident and insurance scams."

# CHAPTER 27

## QUITTERS

**WHEN WE ARRIVED** at work the following day, Ruth handed me two call slips and told me Mr. Clean was anxious to see me. Entering my office, I could see Ruth hadn't made my pot of double roast yet, and I chastised myself for not stopping at the coffee shop downstairs to knock back a double-shot of espresso with two packets of raw sugar. "Ruth, I see the donuts, but no coffee?" I shouted.

"Press the damn button. It's all set up and ready to go," she yelled back. The exchange caused Linda to rush in and prompt a "Sorry, Ruth. Thank you." out of me.

After giving me the evil eye, Linda explained yesterday's announcement had everyone on edge. I pressed the button and stood by, cup in hand. Manny stuck his head in and asked, "Good morning, Boss, spare a minute?"

My "Grab a seat. What's up?" caused Linda to turn toward the exit.

He paused, stepping aside to allow Linda to pass and leave the door open. "That's what a lot of us want to know. Word is you're leaving."

"That hasn't been decided yet. I announced yesterday I'm not doing criminal investigations, body guarding, and security gigs. Linda doesn't want me doing casework anymore, afraid I'll get hurt. It'll be up to the partners if there's a place for me here."

He grimaced and shook his head, saying, "But you're the boss!"

"No free rides, Emanuel. Everyone here contributes to the bottom line," I said. "I spent most of my life kicking ass, taking names, and pissing people off. A lot of people push back, and that scares Linda, big time now that we have a baby. She'd prefer I sold insurance, real estate, or even shoes. What it comes down to is I don't want to screw up another marriage."

"I get it, Boss, but I don't have to like it. If you leave, I'm leaving, too."

"Me too!" Mr. Clean said, stepping through the door and closing it behind. "But you're not leaving, are you?"

"Not yet. We'll see what the partners want me to do. Listen, I don't want to hear folks talking about jumping ship. Linda just doesn't want me working cases. Your end now is more than half our income."

"Potentially, even more. The new guy has a deal he ran across yesterday. What do you think of armored limo service?"

"From what I heard, it makes a lot of money for insurance companies," I said, hoping to shoot it down. He went on, anyway, pointing out the billing possibilities. But he got the message when I pointed out all the illegal shit that goes on in the back of limos. "But don't discourage your guy."

When they left my office, I picked up the phone and dialed the number on the first of the call slips. *"Federal Bureau of Investigation, if you know your party's extension, enter the four digits now. If not, please remain on the line for the next available operator. You are third in line."* I guessed not all the agents were tied up sorting through the stuff captured in the Mar-a-Lago raid. I took a deep breath and entered Agent Green's number. She answered on the second ring. "Agent Green speaking."

"Roland Michaels returning your call."

"The Bureau of Prisons tells us your name came up in a recorded conversation between federal prisoner Vincenzo Costello and his wife. Suspected OC hit man, Sean 'Soldier Boy' Mahan was also mentioned. Have you had contact with Angela Costello or Mahan recently?"

"Why does the FBI have me flagged?"

"Answer my question first."

"No."

"No, you won't answer the question or no to my question?"

"No contact with Mahan or Mrs. Costello."

"We had a query from LAPD if you were on FBI radar recently. Sound right to you?"

"Sure does. My ex-wife was on trial for the attempted murder of her boyfriend last month. Her cousin, Angie, is Big Vinnie's wife and godmother to our kids. But you know all that since I was swept up in the New York office's raid on the Costello home over two years ago. A little homework into my ex's case will put everything in place for you." And we exchanged goodbyes.

The other slip had me calling LAPD Captain Corinne Malinka. I wondered why she didn't call my cell, something official, I guessed. I played along and went through the screening drill and was put on hold. I pictured her gathering around a couple of her minions before picking up and putting me on speaker.

"It's official, Mr. Michaels, Detective Joseph Roberts has officially retired from the Los Angeles Police Department and is no longer subject to department rules and regulations."

"Thank you, Captain. I have taken appropriate actions. I'm counting on the department to prevent future harassment of my family until the man gets served with a restraining order."

"Yes. Please stay on the line while I put you on hold,"

"Not necessary, Corrine. I assume Lieutenant Dacey is on the line. My attorney will be seeking a restraining order against Roberts. Which one of you wants to testify at the hearing?"

"Hi, Rollo," Dacey acknowledged his presence. "I'll be glad to do it, Rollo, since Captain Malinka's upward mobility is still viable, mine ending years ago with my Trump bumper sticker incident."

"Thanks, Bill." I said, "We all know their humor dies when they promote to commander." Putting the Trump bumper sticker on Commander Phipps, aka Numb Nuts' car went south for Bill when Internal Affairs identified his fingerprints on the sticky side. How Phipps got the nickname is the subject of LAPD lore, something to do with a Taser and a partner with poor aim. Many suspected otherwise.

# CHAPTER 28

## SURVEILLANCE

**JOE ROBERTS WAS** served the restraining order on Thursday. The tracker I placed on his car showed him drive by my house in Reseda at 10:20 Friday morning and Marie's house twenty minutes later. Security footage couldn't ID the driver or plate number at either location, but it was enough for me to put a tail on Joe. How long I could afford it was Art's first question.

"I think he's planning something," I said.

Roberts made a couple of stops after the drive-bys, and now the tracker showed his SUV was at his residence. I came up with a plan for the weekend: Around-the-clock surveillance isn't cheap, so I'd do most of it. Clancy would take the four to midnight shift tonight, and I would relieve him and do a twelve-hour stint, with

Manny taking over at noon, Clancy back at midnight, and me next. If he approached my house or Marie's, we'd drop a dime and let the police handle it.

By Sunday afternoon, the battery pack on the tracker I'd placed in Joe's ride must have died or broken loose. Since Joe hadn't made any more passes by the houses, I decided against replacing the battery pack in Gunn's tracker. I thought the wily Roberts now parked on his front lawn, most likely to accommodate security cameras. Self-doubt started creeping in. The possibility of a man with his experience spotting a tail was not out of the question. *Had I underestimated him?*

O  O  O

On Monday morning, Linda and I were called out of the weekly meeting by Ruth. The two of us were surprised by a beaming Diana Wright with my giggling grandchild, Leigh, in her arms.

"I have wonderful news. Laura is coming home tomorrow," she gushed as Leigh squirmed to be set down. Di complied, and Leigh waddled to me with outstretched arms.

"That's wonderful, Di," Linda said while Ruth and Manny stood by, waiting for introductions. I scooped my granddaughter up, kissed her, and did the honors.

The insanity of the Covid plague meant Laura wouldn't be allowed visitors at home for another two weeks, and Di would serve as the at-home caregiver, chief cook, and bottle washer while Laura's husband stayed with his parents for a couple of weeks. Later that afternoon, Linda and

I visited Laura in her isolation room at the hospital. As luck would have it, we got to meet her husband there, too. He was at the hospital the day we did the bone marrow transplant, but we never connected, which Linda felt odd at the time. My mantra, "Shit happens," failed to appease her then. But today, the guy showered me with kudos and appreciation, placating my wife.

My mantra bit me again that night during dinner. Marie called, saying the police stopped by the house to tell her they'd be ending the extra drive-by patrols, starting tomorrow. "What's that about?" she asked.

I had no clue and said I'd call Malinka in the morning to find out. Of course, Marie wasn't happy, even complaining the Smith & Wesson Chief Special I left with her the other night only held five rounds. By reiterating my warning to keep our son away from the gun, I angered her enough to end the call.

o   o   o

Tuesday, Linda stayed home with her mom and Marlowe while I went to the salt mine to meet with my other partners and discuss the future of Michaels & Associates. But first, I needed to call Captain Malinka at Valley Homicide to find out why LAPD was backing away.

After she didn't answer her cell, I called her office. Her adjutant told me she was at a meeting, so I requested a callback. While I waited for Malinka's call, I started to make a list of my equity in this enterprise. When it came right down to it, I wasn't cutting a big hog in the ass, a base salary of $500/week, a 100K insurance policy, and a luxury auto for my ego. Sure, 30% of the net profits were mine each year, 21K last year, but there were none in the first couple. There isn't much equity in used office furniture, computers, electronics, etc. The guns were mine. Goodwill? Just a fantasy.

Art and Clancy had over a week to chew on it. Linda already let them know we were a team: if I go, she'd only stick around to bring Ruth up to speed before joining me in seeking new horizons. Well into our seventh and potentially most successful year, we were comfortable with each other, our strengths and weaknesses, quirks, and biases. Friends when we started, friends we'd remain, I would have no problem with any decision Art and Clancy made. If we all walked, Clancy and I would still collect our police pensions, and Art was still a competent lawyer. *"Malinka on line two,"* Ruth squawked on the intercom.

Picking up, I asked, "We alone?"

"Just me, you, and the NSA on my cell."

"A radio car from Mission Division stopped by my ex's house last night to tell her no more extra patrols. WTF, Corrie?"

"I got the word from on high this morning. Called into the bureau chief's office for a twenty-minute dressing down and grilling about my relationship with persona non grata Roland Michaels."

"Joe's stirring up a shit storm. You okay, Corinne?"

Her "Yeah. I'm fine" didn't match what I knew about LAPD politics. There'd be dozens of captains enjoying her discomfort as they clawed over the competition to reach the top.

There would be no meet with Clancy and Art this day. Art went on a sales call with the new guy to close a 24-7 high-rise building security gig in West Hollywood and Clancy was searching for another runaway. Moneymakers while I spent my time covering my ass.

On my way home, I stopped by Pete Gunn's shop to pick up a new battery pack for the tracker. He had initially said the battery in the tracker unit would last thirty hours, eating up about ten minutes of battery life each time checked. He equated that to more than 180 location checks between three or four weeks. I was pissed the one he gave me only lasted half that. He gave me a new unit. This GPS tracker would map the GPS on my phone with a continuous reading whenever the ignition was on. You could dial it up and get its location anywhere there was cell service. But, he cautioned, it was designed to run off the car's twelve-volt system and showed me how to hook it to the wires leading to the taillights. He suggested sticking it on the rear frame about two feet in and attaching the alligator clips to the taillight wires. He then programmed my cell and the new tracker. "If you can recover the old one, there will be no charge for the upgrade. Sorry, Rollo. I don't know why the battery failed."

"Can you tap into his Wi-Fi and security setups?"

"If you know his password, we can do it now," he said and had me shake my head. "If not, do you know his phone number and email address?"

"Nope, but I can get it, I think," I said and took out my wallet to offer him a Benjamin or two. Now he showed me his version of negative body language.

# CHAPTER 29

## TRAPPED

**WHEN I GOT** home, I discovered we had uninvited company. The question was why. They sat in their plain wrapper car with city plates parked at the curb. When I pulled into the driveway, the two detectives got out of their car, sans jackets. Their ties were askew and collars unbuttoned, Glock 19s holstered on their belts for all the world to see.

"Hey, Michaels. Got a minute?" the alpha shouted from the street.

I forced a smile, faked a look at my watch, and said, "Always got time for my brothers in blue," I said, forcing a smile. They strode up the drive, a tactical two arm lengths between them. I leaned against my Escalade and crossed my arms in front of me, stopping them in their tracks—Alpha, ten feet from me; Beta, fifteen, with his hand on his gun.

"You carrying?" Alpha asked.

"Yes," I said, lowering my hands to my sides and no longer relaxing against my car. "What's this all about?"

"I'll get to that, but we'd feel better talking with you if you weren't armed," he said as Beta slid to his left for a better shooting position. I wondered what bullshit these two had been fed, and by who?

"That's not happening," I said. "Your department has been advised not to question me without my attorney present. I don't know what you two have been told, but before you step into a bucket of shit, you should know all this is being videoed. You are now providing more fodder for my lawsuit."

Beta pulled his gun out, pointed the business end at me, and said, "Turn around. Put your hands on the hood of your car."

"No!" I said, watching Alpha grin. "The hood's too hot. The proper command would be, 'Put your hands on your head, asshole!'"

The screen door flew open, and Linda stepped onto the porch, our daughter in her arms. "What's going on?"

"Freeze!" Beta shouted, spinning toward her with his Glock pointed her way.

"No, Wilson!" Alpha barked. I sprang, grabbed Beta's gun hand with my right, and landed a left hook to his ear, putting him down for the count as his Glock skidded across the blacktop.

Linda's scream of "NO!" and Marlowe's wail froze my leg in the air as I readied to stomp the asshole who pointed a gun at my wife and baby.

Alpha pushed past me, checked his partner, and picked up the Glock, putting it in his waistband. "You going peacefully, or does this get uglier when I call for backup?"

"You know how photogenic I am on the six o'clock news? I wasn't bullshitting about the video. Your partner's action will wind up making you look bad. Why not just leave, maybe get fuckup here checked out? I take it this wasn't an authorized follow-up."

"What are you going to do with the video?"

"Insurance," I said and waved at a couple of neighbors who came out armed with phones to see about all the fuss and shouting.

We helped Wilson to his feet, and his partner guided him to their car. Linda rushed to my side, and we watched them drive off. A half minute later, a patrol car pulled up and said he received a fight call at our location.

"You're late, officers. A couple of detectives broke it up and left a few minutes ago," I said.

And Linda cried, "When's this going to end, Rollo? When?"

O   O   O

I tried sneaking out of the house a bit after 2:00 a.m., only to get busted by Linda. She's been on edge since the shoot-out, and I feared pushing her over it. You'd think by now, I've learned that keeping stuff from her only gets me deeper in trouble. She entered the living room as I put the new tracker into my backpack. Seeing me dressed for stealth mode let her know I was making another run on Joe Roberts.

"I couldn't sleep. Joe Roberts's tracker died, so I need to install a new one on his car. I was going to tell you, but you were asleep."

Her inner lie detector had her shaking her head, and anger flashed on her face. "Bullshit. I was awake."

I gave her my new concerns spurred by my latest conversations with Marie and Malinka. I showed her the new tracker and explained how the magnets made this installation less risky than last week. I held back on the info about the photo gallery on Joe's fridge. Our conversation woke up Marlowe, so I gave Linda a hug and said, "I'll be back in a couple of hours."

Linda's car seemed appropriate since the North Hollywood patrol units probably had my Escalade on a BOLO. Again, I parked around the corner from Joe's house. This time a fire hydrant provided the only parking space available. I was sure no parking checkers were writing tickets at 3:20 in the morning.

There was no rain to cover my tracks and muffle my sounds this time. I hadn't counted on the dogs. The clear night air meant the family pets weren't all housed safely from the elements. By the time Joe's hovel was in sight, the alert was being barked through the neighborhood by at least a half-dozen hounds from hell. I contemplated aborting but reasoned Joe was spending another night in booze-induced slumber.

I clung to the shadows where I could and swiftly traversed the patches lit by street lights. The four-minute walk had me crouching at the driver's side of Joe's SUV.

If the shit hit the fan, I was sure I could sprint to Linda's car in a minute. I slipped out of my backpack, got the new tracker and pen light, and crawled under Joe's ride. The magnets clicked as I stuck the device to the gas tank. The taillight wires were where Pete told me, and the alligator clips made quick work of the installation. No muss, no fuss, no tape. Now, I wiggled over to recover the old tracker from the axle. Shit! It was gone. Somebody had removed the tracker; they even got all the remnants of the duct tape.

And then the house's front door opened, and lights came on. Not just the two dinky porchlights but some bright ones, too. They reached halfway under the passenger side of the SUV. I shrank from them like a vampire does sunlight.

"I knew you'd be back for your tracker, asshole," Joe Roberts said as I scrambled to get out from under the vehicle. Joe's size ten Red Wings soon filled my little view of the world, keeping me under his car. I crawled back to the other side. Again, he was there, kicking at my head to keep me from escaping.

"You might find what I'm about to do shocking, Michaels, but I've been storing up a lot of energy with the hope of expending it on you. You remember these toys the department issued us?" he said, showing me a Taser gun. Then he pulled the trigger and lit me up. When the zapping ended, I still was twitching. He dragged me out by my hair and hoodie like I was a wet towel. The last I heard was Joe's taunting laughter and the barking of dogs as he choked me out.

# CHAPTER 30

## TOTALLY FUCKED

**I OPENED MY** eyes to darkness, gripped by nausea and pain. A radio played loudly somewhere in the dark. The unmistakable smell of urine and feces and the sour taste of vomit assaulted my senses. I was cold and naked, my hands and feet hog-tied behind me. My head throbbed as I separated my face from the cold floor. I tried to sit up only to bang my head on something very hard above me. Dizziness made my stomach retch with dry heaves as I fell back down onto my other side. Across the floor, a thin line of light was barely visible, as if the source was on the other side of a door. *Where the fuck am I?*

"Hello?…Hello?" I croaked, my mouth too dry for talk. I worked up some saliva and shouted out another "Hello!" The radio went silent. My "Hey!" had the door open, and the backlit shadow of a man didn't quite reach me where I lay.

"Good, you're alive, asshole. Thought you might die before I had my fun with you," the unmistakable voice of Joe Roberts said, causing a kaleidoscope of disjointed images to fill my brain. I fought them back to use the light from the doorway to ascertain my surroundings and circumstances.

I was in a bathroom, chained to a sink fixture, a commode to my left, and a shower enclosure to my right. The walls looked to be rough-hewn logs with plaster or mortar seams. It made sense; Joe had a cabin retreat in Big Bear, often bragging about his deer hunting prowess. I now knew where I was but still was clueless about how I got here. "Why am I here, Joe?"

"So I can watch you die," he said. "Try to get some rest, Michaels. I have a big day planned for us tomorrow. Can I get you anything before I go?"

"Couple of aspirin?"

"Sorry, fresh out. Anything else?"

I couldn't make out his facial expressions, but knowing him as I do, I was sure he was smirking. "Water?"

"My dog used to lap it out of the toilet. You can do the same. Sweet dreams," he said, stepping back to close the door.

"Why wait 'til tomorrow? Why not kill me now?"

"Who said anything about killing you? Sure, you're going to beg me to do it, but what's the fun in that? I promise you're going to wish you were never born before I'm done!" he shouted, his voice rising with each word, his fists shaking in rage.

"You never killed anybody in your life, Joe, so why now? Is this still about some piece of ass ten years ago?"

He rushed back in and started to put the boots to me, spewing every cuss word he knew. I rolled up under the sink, but the only cover I could find was my back. The last I remembered was the taste of blood in my mouth before I slipped into unconsciousness.

I didn't know how many hours passed, but a faint glow of daylight was visible through the opened bathroom door. Had Joe not closed it? Was he still here? "Hey, Joe!" I called out. He didn't answer. "Joe?" Maybe he slept.

As the quiet minutes passed, more light spilled into my prison to reveal my blood had pooled around where my face had spent the dark hours. How many times had I slipped in and out of consciousness? Or was I dreaming? My body registered pain just about everywhere but my hands and feet, which were numb and felt swollen. My tongue pressed up against a couple of loose lower teeth and a lacerated swollen lower lip. He obviously wasn't wearing slippers when he was kicking me.

Anger took over and propelled me out from under the sink and onto my knees. Roberts had handcuffed me behind my back. A nylon rope secured my feet to the cuffs, and a length of chain was wrapped around the sink's two-inch drain pipe and attached to the cuffs. A mirror hung a foot above the back of the sink. If I could break it, a piece of its glass could cut the ropes tying my feet to the handcuffs behind me. I struggled through unspeakable pain, twisting my body to get to the mirror. It proved an impossible task, and I sank to the floor in painful defeat, cursing Joe Roberts as frustration devoured my soul.

Then, I prayed: *God grant me the serenity to accept the things I cannot change, the courage to change the things I can, and the wisdom to know the difference.* And then the kaleidoscope of images I had repressed hours ago started to play in my head. I forced myself to watch.

First, I saw myself hugging Linda. She walked away with her shoulders slumped after I'd disappointed her again.

Next, I was under Joe's SUV, being Tasered, paralyzed but conscious, Joe talking to me unintelligibly. The world moved as a hand dragged me out from under the car by my hair. I tried to get free, but an arm went around my neck. I knew what was coming and gasped a deep breath before my lights went out.

Next thing I know, I'm under a canvas tarp, in the back of a moving vehicle, trussed up like a turkey, with my mouth taped shut. The car radio is on FM105, telling Southern California it was 6:05 in the morning. The DJ was soon playing Cheap Trick's songs from the '80s, the bass player and drummer firing every synopsis in my brain. It all seemed to mean something to Joe as he sang along to their Dream Police number.

An hour later, Joe announced, "I need to piss. How about you?" We pulled into *I don't know and don't care.* He popped the hatch, pulled back the tarp, and stuck a needle in my leg. "This synthetic Chinese opioid is some tricky shit that could kill you if I'm not careful." He laughed. "I see you already used the facilities. You're out of control, Michaels." And the tarp went back over me, and he closed the hatch. Maybe five minutes later, we were back on the road, and I soon nodded off, only to awaken in this hellhole where Joe held me.

The slideshow was over, and the realization that I was totally fucked set in, and tears blurred my vision. *"Wah-wah-waah. You hurt or just feeling sorry for yourself, Maggot?"* my drill sergeant shouted in my inner ear. *"You want me to call your mama, boy, or are you gonna man up?"*

"Yes, Sergeant!" I shouted and got back up on my knees to try the mirror again. That's when I saw what I failed to see the first time. A drinking glass sat in the rusted toothbrush holder screwed to the wall. How had I missed it? Was it there before? Is it really there now?

I contorted my body past snap-crackle-pop and got my damaged teeth clamped on the rim of the glass. It was real! I lowered it to the floor, forced my hands to grip the chain, and broke the glass. Using a shard, I sawed on the rope for what seemed an hour but most likely only ten to fifteen minutes. Cutting through one strand allowed my bloody fingers to uncoil the damn thing, freeing my swollen feet from my hands. I was spent from the effort and hurt like hell but recalled the DI's admonition to *"Man up!"* and swung my legs out in front of me.

"Aargh!" It wasn't pretty. My size 11 Ds looked to be 13 EEEs. Half-inch-deep furrows encircled my ankles. The bruising started mid-calf, the discoloration darkening as it went down to my toes, red to purple to black. I rolled to my side to do my handcuff escape trick, knowing full well that without the key I wouldn't complete it.

My screams of pain seemed to help me scoot the cuffs under my ass, but getting my legs through was pure agony. I laid there, catching a breather, mouth dry, throat raw, and smiled, thinking, *Won't Joe be surprised.*

*"Okay, Maggot, break's over. Time to get you hydrated!"* the DI barked in my head. I used the sink to pull myself from the floor, my knees complaining all the way. My dead feet felt nothing, unable to communicate with my brain, requiring me to hang on to the sink to keep from falling. I cranked the handle marked C, and the faucet hissed for a few seconds before spewing some rusty water. I let it run for a half-minute more and heard a well-pump come on somewhere, increasing the flow. I rinsed the blood from my swollen hands, cupped them together, and drank handfuls of cool metal-flecked water about half of it running down the front of my nude body.

Bright daylight filled the outer room, pouring into the windowless bathroom. The added light allowed me a better look at my face in the mirror since the light hanging from the ceiling didn't have a pull cord. Not pretty. Joe had done a number on me—one eye barely opened, lump on the outside of the other, fat lip, bloody gums, and bent nose. A two-inch laceration, starting in the middle of my forehead and running into my hairline, oozed and scabbed. I felt other bumps on my head but no open wounds.

If I were to survive, I'd need to kill this son of a bitch!

# CHAPTER 31

## ESCAPE PLANS

**I NEEDED A** plan of attack and escape. I thought it odd that Joe would leave me to my own devices, but how do you figure crazy? I had to be quick because the psycho bastard could walk in the door anytime. His threat about "a big day planned for us" was probably something I could live without.

One of my military and police training tenets was to be aware of your surroundings. I took a tentative step away from the sink that was supporting me for the past ten minutes. Pins and needles had replaced the numbness in my feet, but vertigo forced me to grab hold of the sink again. Thankfully, a couple of deep breaths and a few blinks made the dizziness disappear. The running water, and my gulping a bunch of it, made me stagger to the commode to relieve myself first. I guessed the small bathroom to be no more than a six-by-eight box, and Joe's dog chain would allow me to explore every square foot of it. As I did my thing in the toilet bowl, it was apparent that Joe's housekeeping skills were nil, with the stains and murk telling me why Joe's dog wasn't around. When I pulled the chain to flush, the overhead toilet tank gave me hope and inspiration. Was it possible its lid would provide me a weapon to bash in Joe's skull? Too bad it was just out of my reach. Could that be the reason there was no toilet seat and cover? No way. The overlooked glass in the toothbrush holder proved Joe wouldn't think of that.

Two feet with little or no feeling and a concussed brain made balancing on the edges of the commode a big challenge. Neither the waterline feed to the tank nor the flimsy flush chain offered any help, so I took hold of the two-inch pipe running from the tank to the bowl, pulled myself up onto the rim, and used the wall to steady myself. I couldn't grab hold of the porcelain lid with one hand, so I pushed it off with the hand that didn't have a death grip on the pipe to keep me upright.

The lid crashed to the floor, exploding like a bomb. I got down from my perch, hoping one of the pieces would be large enough for my intended purpose. Sitting on the bowl's edge, I picked up the only large piece, guessing it weighed close to three pounds, with a cleaved edge that could do significant damage. The question now was how to get close enough to strike the bastard. Ambush was impossible. There was no place to hide. And he and I were trained: Always check the hands! Joe would see I was not hog-tied.

I clung to my ceramic club, went to the doorway to the cabin's great room, and stuck my head out. The door to freedom was twelve feet to my right between two large windows. The wall facing me was maybe twelve feet from the bathroom. A large stone fireplace took up about a third of it. A large ten-by-eighteen carpet covered most of the wood floor. The areas on either end of the bathroom probably contained a small kitchen on one side and a bedroom on the other. But none of this info helped my plan.

All the exertion was catching up to me. I estimated I was Joe's prisoner for more than a day now. It looked to be midafternoon, probably for only thirty-six hours, unless he kept me unconscious with Fentanyl for more than a day. Being thirsty but not hungry made that a good possibility. I returned to the sink and worked on my thirst with Joe's skanky water, probably pumped from a cistern filled with rainwater from his roof. And where was Joe? Maybe back in La-La Land, covering his tracks. I put the club under the sink and laid down to regain energy from the stored fat around my middle that I usually dressed to conceal. A vision of a Tommy's Burger flashed, but I toughed it out. I dozed off to dreams of coffee and maple glazed donuts and people knocking on my office door and calling my phone, wanting some. Good thing I locked the door.

Sadly, I woke up. Not in my office but on a floor between a sink and a seat-less commode in a cold cabin, needing to pee. The orange glow of sunlight told me the night was fast approaching in these mountains. I checked behind me, finding my improvised weapon. Its heft bolstering my feelings of empowerment. I gleefully envisioned the sharp edge coming down hard, splitting Joe's head like a melon.

I staggered to the door and proudly pissed on Joe's carpet. The little victories were adding up, spurring me on. Leaning against the doorjamb, I spotted a wall switch to the right of the door. When I flicked it on, the bare bulb light above the sink behind me came on. This caused me to notice the orange glow in the cabin had turned to gray, and the whole place would soon be in total darkness, except for a bare 40-watt bulb above a grime-coated sink. I was alarmed by the discoveries of the water glass, the light switch, and not being mindful of time passing. My cognitive abilities were no doubt impaired. "Don't let doubt defeat you!" Sun Tzu's *The Art of War* got me past it.

I had to assume that by yesterday morning, Linda had hit the panic button because I hadn't returned from my covert mission. It wouldn't be the first time I got home late, but she broke me of the "not calling" habit during our pregnancy. What would she do? Hopefully, alert our partners and be guided by their responses. Logic brought me to believe Art, Clancy, and the crew were out and about looking for leads and were all over anything Joe Roberts for clues. Is that why Joe isn't here, reveling in my torture?

# CHAPTER 32

## SWEET DREAMS

**I WAS RUNNING** out of gas, my body ached, and my thoughts were muddled. My makeshift weapon seemed to be gaining weight with the passing of each minute. So, I propped it next to where I stood, slid down the wall directly under the light switch, and sat on my ass. Although I took pride in my ability to think on my feet, this was where I did most of my best thinking. My stamina was into a half-life mode: each burst of energy lasting half as long as the one before it; each subsequent rest period taking twice as long. Lack of food? I've gone longer than three days during survival training.

Could this mean I'd been in Joe's clutches at least twenty-four hours longer than I thought? Fentanyl? Yep. Zapped, then dosed, cuffed, and trussed. Then he dosed me again in the back of his SUV during his potty break. I remember being fully clothed in the ride up here. He must have cut the clothes off my body rather than risk untying me when we arrived. How much dope had he given me?

I limped over to the sink on unsteady legs to use the sink light and examine my body for puncture wounds. From what I knew from my time working at Narcotics, the average addict shot up twice a day, increasing the dosage, but not the frequency, as his habit needed more and more dope to attain the same sought-after high.

I had used Demerol a number of times for pain. The pain I felt now meant Joe hadn't dosed me for at least twelve hours, likely longer. I found three needle marks, two on my thigh and one on my left shoulder. Two I could account for, and the third had me clueless. Knowing I couldn't see some parts of my torso, there could be more. I could have been tied up longer. Thoughts of food snuck in, but pain and plenty of water held hunger pangs at bay. Exhaustion was now my main concern. The dark circles around my eyes were more than just bruising. There was no humor in the face of the clown looking back at me in the mirror; in fact, he could be a character in a horror movie. Maybe I could scare Joe Roberts to death? Maybe twenty winks were all I needed to clear my head. Perhaps this is all a dream. Maybe…

*Linda and I rubbed tanning lotion on each other, planning to sun ourselves on towel-covered chaise lounges by the side of our pool. Her mom sat in the palm tree shade on the other side, with our baby daughter in her arms. Marlowe drank hungrily from her bottle, safe in Grandma's arms, eyes closed, and not a care in the world.*

*My mischievous son, Brandon, swam underwater, looking to dump his older sister off her float as she soaked up the rays. I could hear the theme from* Jaws *playing somewhere in the background. Then Joe Roberts came through the gate dressed up as Pool Guy, and the float flipped over, and Melissa screamed, and Linda shouted my name, and Joe Tasered the living shit out of me.* I knew the dream was over as I lay stunned on the floor. As urine puddled beneath me, the now familiar walls of my prison pulsated with each beat of my heart.

"Well, ain't you some kind of special asshole," Joe snickered, plunging the contents of a syringe into my side. "Sweet dreams, Michaels, and don't hurt yourself. That's my job." He hit the light switch and closed the door, leaving me in darkness. The little sliver of light from under the door reminded me I was helpless, and my darkest hours were yet to come. Even opioid-induced dreams wouldn't assuage my feelings of failure and guilt for coming so close and yet being so far away.

O   O   O

I awoke, shivering behind a plastic curtain, no longer chained beneath the sink. Again, my hands were cuffed behind my back; the dog chain was now double-wrapped around my neck, running behind me and through the cuffs, and fastened somewhere above me. Dim lighting suggested a closet, but as I craned my neck to look upward, I could see I was still in the bathroom, this time in Joe's shower.

I felt very little pain, probably the drugs the bastard gave me. I noticed he hadn't bothered securing my feet. I stood on unsteady legs in the compact shower stall and pushed the curtain open with my foot. The light spilling into the bathroom seemed to be dimming, indicating it was late afternoon. Again, thirst overtook me. I turned the single valve a half turn left and was rewarded with a small trickle that splashed my face before lining up with my open mouth. While drinking, I saw that Joe had anchored the chain around my neck to the showerhead. Hmmm… Even Houdini couldn't slip the cuffs and chain without strangling himself. I wondered if my legs could jump a foot high. Could the pipe support what was left of me? I shut the water off and took a practice jump of maybe four or five inches. Plan B was in order. Pushing off the back wall could double the force of my two hundred pounds. Would successive jolts weaken the fixture to the breaking point? Would the noise wake Joe up? Is he here?

Hearing a car pulling to the front of the cabin made me try. The chain tore into my flesh, the plastic shower stall reverberating like a drum. *Bam! Bam!*

"What the fuck!" Joe shouted, sounding pissed and half-awake.

And then I gave him another *bam!* The third time was not the charm and I was spent. My neck was raw, blood oozed from my collarbone area, and I sank to the floor, watching my blood go down the drain with the water that now dripped from the showerhead.

Then someone pounded on the cabin door. I rose to my feet and screamed. The loudest scream of my life propelled me forward and tore the showerhead out of the wall.

# CHAPTER 33

## RESCUE

**"POLICE! OPEN THE** door!" someone yelled as I untangled the chain around my neck and slid my cuffed hands to my front. The sound of shattering glass and breaking wood preceded Joe Roberts positioning himself in the bathroom doorway, gun in hand. He was smiling as he raised the automatic in my direction. I rushed him, swinging the showerhead still attached to the chain like some medieval warrior swinging a mace. His eyes flashed to the front of the cabin as he fired four rounds at me. I let my flail fly and missed. The burning in my side meant he didn't. And I hit the floor in case there was more coming.

All hell broke loose. No longer firing at me, Joe twitched and jerked, as he kept firing at whoever took down the cabin door. And then his head exploded, and he slid down the doorjamb, slumped on the threshold of hell. My tormentor wound up facing me with his eyes frozen open. I could only hope I was the last thing he saw as he left this world.

I lay on the dirty floor waiting for my rescuers to rush in but only heard moaning. I staggered to my feet, stepped over a very dead Joe Roberts, and stuck my head around the corner. "Shit!" I uttered and rushed to my partner, Clancy. He lay on the floor under the smashed window. Blood seeped through his fingers as he clutched the left side of his chest. His other hand had a hole in it with some bones sticking out. Then the Mounties roared up, lights blazing.

"Ambulance," I shouted. "My partner's been hit." One deputy talked into his body microphone, and the other drew his sidearm. Clancy's eyes flittered, and I said, "Stay with me, Pard."

"Where's the shooter?" the deputy, with his gun in hand, asked.

"Dead," I answered. "Inside by the bathroom door." And off he went, his partner rushing to me.

"I...I hit him twice...the crazy fucker...he kept on shooting," Clancy said, coughing up a bright red foam.

"Easy, Pard, you got him good," I said, watching the deputy tuck Clancy's Glock into his own waistband. "ETA on the rescue unit?" I asked.

"Twenty," he said. "We need to stop the bleeding. I got a first aid kit in the trunk," he said, and ran off to the back of his cruiser. Clancy's eyes fluttered, and I noticed he was leaking from his back also, a small puddle of blood pooling on the floor under his shoulder. The deputy was back and opened the large kit with a red cross emblazoned on its lid. He quickly had scissors snipping through Clancy's clothing, telling me to get out of the way so his partner could help. I hobbled out of their way and watched them work, sure they would save him.

Joe's bullet entered below Clancy's breast, hit a rib, and came out the back next to my partner's shoulder blade. The entry wound was a third of the size the round made coming out, but the deputies treated both holes the same, stuffing each with gauze and covering them with wide strips of tape for an airtight seal. They then wrapped his wounded hand with gauze and him with a blanket.

I was next. "First things first. Get these cuffs off me!" And they did.

I also had a through and through GSW. Mine, a flesh wound in some excess girth I'd been putting on since marrying Linda. Luckily, Joe missed my one kidney that was leaking blood only a few weeks ago. My wound only warranted one strip of tape, six inches long, to cover the ins and outs of getting shot. The ambulance crew scrounged up another blanket when they arrived. It turns out my shivering didn't have much to do about being cold. I would continue to shake well into the night.

While we waited for the ambulance crew to check vitals and get Clancy on their gurney, I gave one of the deputies a rundown of my captivity. He told me he and his partner had been dispatched to this location yesterday to check for a missing person named Roland Mitchel or if anyone here knew his whereabouts. I just closed my eyes and shook my head. I wanted to scream but had nothing left. Clancy loaded, I was assisted into the ambulance and we sped away, leaving the two deputies to await their detectives and the coroner.

My first call was to Linda, thanks to the friendly ambulance driver who let me use his cell. The wailing siren had me explain that Clancy was injured while rescuing me, and I was riding with him to the hospital. She wasn't happy with my answers to her rapid-fire questioning. My "I'll keep you posted" pissed her off even worse. "I'm sorry, sweetheart, I really have to go," hurt me more than Joe's bullet.

Then I called Art and gave him the skinny of what went down. He agreed to get Linda, Sylvia, and himself to the hospital by morning. Before returning the ambulance driver's phone, I noted the date and time: Tuesday, 6:48 p.m. I'd been Joe's prisoner for over three days. Humiliated, tortured, and dehumanized by the maniac who is now dead. Now there could be no payback. No revenge! How do I live with that?

For the next two nights, Clancy and I shared a ground-floor room at Bear Lake Community Hospital because it was a one-story facility with limited space. But size isn't everything. Our treatment was top-notch, and the staff was great, despite all the interruptions. One TV to a room had me pull rank to get control of the remote. The local news out of San Bernardino mentioned a shootout in a cabin by Big Bear Lake, leaving one dead and two wounded. Sketchy, as if somebody was keeping the lid on. Today, we're out of here. I'm going home, chauffeured by Linda. And Clancy to UCLA Hospital with Sylvia via ambulance.

Joe Roberts had gone bat shit crazy on both of us. According to the San Bernardino Homicide Dicks, Joe sprayed eleven, and Clancy got off four in the shootout. That's fifteen rounds in less than ten seconds. I caught one, Clancy two, and Joe three. Since mine was a through-and-through not recovered, the detectives speculated that Clancy fired the round going through my love handle. We went over my observations a few more times. Finally, I told them they were idiots unless my partner had magic bullets. I was shot probably before Clancy even drew his Glock. I saw Joe fire at least four at me in rapid succession, not knowing which one of his last two caused my wound. The crazy bastard must have wanted me dead, real bad, shooting me first when Clancy was kicking in the door at Joe's Big Bear hideaway.

No doubt Clancy would be dead if he weren't smart enough to notify the San Bernardino Sherriff's Station before busting in. As it played out, I was the only one standing when the two deputies arrived. I'm sure they'll be talking about the shit show they discovered for years to come.

I was most concerned about Clancy. My hero was hit twice while putting two shots in Joe's upper body with a third going through his neck, blowing his spine out the back of his head. The .9mm round piercing Clancy's lung didn't blow it out, proving POTUS wrong again. But the other wound significantly damaged a bunch of bones in my partner's hand. The UCLA hand specialists will have their work cut out for them in its reconstruction.

LAPD detectives from their elite Robbery Homicide Unit showed up the second day. The San Berdu guys gave them a courtesy tour of the shooting scene and copies of all the reports before they got to us at the hospital. Art introduced himself as mine and Clancy's lawyer. Clancy was in no shape for an interview, so that left me. These two were probably fans of their deceased comrade-in-arms now residing in the county morgue. I knew Detective Doug Collins from way back during my time with the LAPD, but not his younger partner, Gillis, or something like that. They started lobbing softballs, like who did what, when, how, and why. Then, integrity questions, qualification to recognize bat shit crazy when I saw it, and other benign bullshit. That out of the way, it was nitty-gritty time, and Doug got right to it.

"So, you admit to having two altercations with Detective Roberts, breaking his arm in the most recent. Then you recently lodged a couple of personnel complaints against him that caused him to retire. And didn't you have sex with his fiancée back in the day? You feel any guilt in pushing him over the edge, Michaels?" the lead detective asked.

"No, Doug. I regret that I wasn't the one who permanently put his lights out." Doug bristled and stepped closer to my bed and took hold of the rails. So I got a little more challenging. "Are you trying to make Roberts a victim here? He went off the rails and threatened my family. Kidnapped and tortured me. I bet the DA will review all his convictions and release a bunch of cons from the joint because of this. He wasn't the man you think he was, Doug!"

Art stepped in to end the interview.

Clancy had feigned sleep while listening to the whole thing. When they left, he said, "I thought you read Dale

Carnegie's *How to Win Friends and Influence People*? By the time they left, I had the distinct impression they wouldn't piss on you if you were on fire."

We all laughed at his lame jokes. Before heading back to Los Angeles, Art reminded us of the seriousness at hand, and the pitfalls of talking to the police. "Refer them to me. It's what you're paying me for!"

"We're paying you?" I asked. He left shaking his head. Clancy and I both knew heeding Art's advice would piss off a lot of Ivory Tower types. The real cops would get it if somebody aired the department's dirty laundry. I had a few friends in the media who were always grateful for a timely tip.

After a worrisome night at the Big Bear Chateau, Linda and Clancy's wife, Sylvia, brought my clothes and some toiletries for my partner. The wives also brought some needed good news: Art hired licensed Private Investigator Alita Combs to "man" the investigative branch of Michaels & Associates during our recovery.

The convoy plan was simple enough: Linda would follow the ambulance to the UCLA Med Center in Santa Monica, me riding shotgun. From there, we'd take the Sepulveda Pass to the Valley and home, avoiding the pain of the 405 Freeway's rush hour traffic. It was the long way home, but our friends were worth every mile. My brother in blue saved me from a terrible death and almost got killed doing it. How do you repay that?

O   O   O

Two weeks later, I'm back to work, mostly watching over Lita Combs's shoulder. Today she is out doing interviews on of all things, a sexual harassment case. What do I know that could be of help to her? So I sit in my office with a fresh cup of dark roast while lost in thoughts of the past, present, and future. My time as a cop was years of wonder for me. You worked with partners, some of whom didn't like you but would back you when the going got tough. Such was the nature of the beast then. The thin blue line stood between the good folk and the assholes. But now, it seemed it was getting more challenging to tell who was who as Wokeism obscured reason.

Harassment at the hands of a few within the organization I'd given my all to was a bitterness I couldn't get out of my mouth. Art thinks the best way my story gets told involves a seven-figure lawsuit, but I fantasize about six-figure book deals. Through all this, my MD wants me to see a therapist. He laughed when I told him I had seen one for a while who ended my court-ordered sessions because I was making *her* crazy.

Last week, the Coroner's Inquest ruled Joe's death a justifiable homicide. Of note to many, the ME discovered a walnut-sized cancerous growth in Joe's frontal lobe believed to have caused him to go off the reservation. We thought it a convenient excuse, and Art was anxious to bring the lawsuit against the city and Joe's estate. But I was hesitant. Linda and I decided not to think about Joe Roberts for a while and take a month off.

Linda entered my office, interrupting my contemplations, "Two agents from the FBI are here to see you."

"And yet again, shit happens!" I said. "Show them in and ask Art to join us."

# EPILOGUE

***IN THE END,*** Joe's story was a sad one. An only child whose parents were teachers in the Los Angeles Unified School system. They ordained Joe to follow in their footsteps and footed the bill for Joe to attend Cal State Northridge. Fate intervened during Joe's senior year when two ex-cons invaded the Roberts home, murdered Joe's parents, and looted the house.

Two months later, and his parents' murders still unsolved, Joe graduated from Cal State. With his degree in hand, he joined LAPD. During his third month in the police academy, two detectives from Robbery/Homicide pulled Joe out of class to identify some property recovered by members of the LAPD's Pawnshop Detail. He quickly recognized his mother's engraved wedding band and matching engagement ring. The homicide detectives then showed Joe a Swiss watch taken from the wrist of the suspect who had pawned the rings. The detectives told him of the DNA match to crime scene evidence. Joe immediately decided what avenues his career path would follow.

Art found out Joe had no living relatives and died intestate. His embittered ex-wife wanted nothing to do with anything Joe. He designated the proceeds of a small insurance policy and the funds in his credit union and deferred compensation accounts to the Los Angeles Police Memorial Fund. In total, a bit over 250K. Clancy and I as ex-cops didn't want to interfere with any of that. But the City's deep pockets and Joe's dilapidated house, as bad as it was, would still fetch a half-mil. And what about that bullet-riddled cabin in Big Bear? All this had Art salivating and Clancy and Sylvia thinking about it. I didn't trust myself to make the right decision and opted for a month of R & R in the Florida Keys. It was time to introduce Marlowe to her other grandmother.

Ruth chauffeured us to the airport for a nonstop to Miami. Our bags checked, our carry-ons both dedicated in support of Marlowe, who became more high-maintenance every day. The TSA screening was as intrusive as ever, yet Marlowe seemed happy with all the attention her slipping Covid mask brought her. Linda was in protective mother mode, refusing anyone to touch our daughter but me and herself. We slowed up the line a bit but did not upset the TSA folks who, by now, have seen everything.

We settled in our seats, me on the window, Linda on the aisle, and Marlowe in her car seat, strapped between us. As we rose over the ocean, I held Linda's hand. We locked eyes and smiled. Calmness took hold of me as the plane started to bank toward the east. A four-week stay filled with leisure awaited to heal body and mind. I knew I was putting PI work behind me, a career I got into to pay alimony and child support. Linda had broken me out of my egocentric ways, making me consider prioritizing my responsibilities. Not only to her and Marlowe, but my three other kids, and yes, even to their mothers.

I happily looked forward to what our next month in Florida had in store for us, but after that? Again, I was clueless.

Warm and Fuzzy

# ABOUT THE AUTHOR

**KIP MEYERHOFF HAS** been a columnist, novelist, and storyteller for most of his adult life. In his memoir, *Cooking with Kip*, he tells how a New York kid with a fondness for cooking and eating wound up on the banks of the Ohio River writing crime stories and cooking columns. Maybe two stints in Uncle Sam's army, a career in law enforcement, and owning a Los Angeles PI business had something to do with it. Or was it his ownership of three restaurants? Food for thought and stories for entertainment? Or vice versa?

# OTHER BOOKS BY KIP MEYERHOFF

Cooking with Kip, A Cook's Memoir
Deadwood and Beyond
The Big Vinnie Chronicles
A Six-Pack to Go